D0572705

"History, despite its wrenching pain, cannot be unlived, but if faced with courage, need not be lived again."

—MAYA ANGELOU

Where Time Stood Still

BETH ADAMS

Guideposts

Danbury, Connecticut

Savannah Secrets is a trademark of Guideposts.

Published by Guideposts Books & Inspirational Media
100 Reserve Road, Suite E200
Danbury, CT 06810
Guideposts.org

Copyright © 2020 by Guideposts. All rights reserved.

This book, or parts thereof, may not be reproduced, stored in a retrieval system, or transmitted in any form or by any means, electronic, mechanical, photocopying, recording, or otherwise, without the written permission of the publisher.

This is a work of fiction. Savannah, Georgia, actually exists, and some places and characters may be based on actual places and people whose identities have been used with permission or fictionalized to protect their privacy. Apart from the actual people, events, and locales that figure into the fiction narrative, all other names, characters, businesses, and events are the creation of the author's imagination and any resemblance to actual persons or events is coincidental.

Every attempt has been made to credit the sources of copyrighted material used in this book. If any such acknowledgment has been inadvertently omitted or miscredited, receipt of such information would be appreciated.

Scripture references are from the following sources: *The Holy Bible, King James Version* (KJV). *The Holy Bible, New International Version* (NIV). Copyright ©1973, 1978, 1984, 2011 by Biblica, Inc. Used by permission of Zondervan. All rights reserved worldwide. www.zondervan.com

Cover and interior design by Müllerhaus
Cover illustration by Pierre Droal, represented by Deborah Wolfe, LTD.
Typeset by Aptara, Inc.

Printed and bound in the United States of America
10 9 8 7 6 5 4 3 2 1

Where Time Stood Still

Chapter One

MEREDITH BELLEFONTAINE FINISHED SCANNING THE stack of claims and closed the folder on her desk. Investigating insurance fraud was exactly as boring as it sounded, as it turned out. It paid the bills, but if she had to scan one more line of medical code right now, her eyes would give out. She needed a break.

Meredith walked out into the hallway and took a mug from the table outside her office.

"More coffee?" Julia Foley called from inside her own office.

"Just one more." Meredith lifted the carafe and poured herself a cup of rich, dark coffee then wandered over to the doorway of Julia's office. The old wooden floorboards creaked under her feet. "Are you having any more fun than I am?"

"For sure. I'm working on our favorite cheating spouse." A map of Savannah was spread out on Julia's desk, and she had highlighted several spots scattered throughout the city.

"You don't *know* that Isabella's cheating," Meredith clarified.

"I don't know for sure," Julia said. "But I have a pretty good idea."

Julia was working on a case that had come their way a few weeks prior. A lawyer she had worked with many years before was handling a divorce for one of the city's wealthiest businessmen, Dennis Healding, and he was hoping to prove that his wife was having an affair. This would mean that the wife, Isabella, wouldn't be entitled to his money, according to the terms of their prenuptial agreement. It was the kind of sordid business that made Meredith even more grateful for the long, happy marriage she and Ron had enjoyed. But, well, like insurance fraud, it paid the bills.

"What are you doing?" Meredith nodded at the map. She heard the front door open, but she knew Carmen was at the front desk, so she focused on Julia.

"Marking off the places she used her credit card," Julia said, pointing at the highlighted areas on the map. "Since Isabella disabled location services on her phone, I'm stuck trying to trace her path by looking at her credit card bills."

It was the kind of tedious work that made up much of the day-to-day running of a private investigation business, and normally Meredith didn't mind. But today she was antsy. Sun streamed in through the large windows, and the oppressive muggy heat of summer had finally given way to cooler temperatures and a bright, sunny late-September day.

"I don't know whether to say I hope you find what you're looking for or not," Meredith said. She always hoped investigations like this came up empty. She always wanted to find that a spouse hadn't been cheating, that it was all a big misunderstanding, and that the marriage might be saved after all.

Julia, a former lawyer and Chatham County judge, was more pragmatic. "I hope I do. I know she's cheating. I can feel it. I just need to find proof."

Meredith took a sip of her coffee and turned when she heard footsteps coming down the hall. It was Carmen, her lush black hair pulled into a ponytail.

"Meredith?" Carmen said. "*¿Tienes un momento?* There's someone here asking for you. She says she's the daughter of a friend of yours."

"Who is it?"

"Her name is Rachel Martin."

It took Meredith a moment to place the name, but then it popped into her head. "Lindy's daughter!"

Meredith had been in a Bible study with Lindy Martin a few years back, and she had enjoyed her wry humor and insightful take on the scriptures. Lindy had talked about her daughter Rachel many times and had asked for prayer for her while she'd gone through a rough patch in college.

"She says she has something she's hoping you can investigate for her."

"As long as it's not insurance fraud or another cheating spouse, send her on back."

"*Sí.*" Carmen turned to go, but then turned back and cocked her eyebrow. "The businessman's wife is totally cheating."

"Told you!" Julia shouted from her office.

Meredith shook her head and waited while Carmen walked back down the hallway and returned a few minutes later with a tall woman in skinny jeans and boots following behind her. The woman had the same aquiline nose and brown hair as her mom. She was probably in her late twenties or early thirties, Meredith guessed.

"Rachel." Meredith smiled.

"Hi there. You must be Mrs. Bellefontaine." Rachel had pale skin and a light sprinkling of freckles over her cheeks.

"Please, call me Meredith." She held out her hand, and Rachel shook it gently. "How is your mother?"

"She's doing fine. The Garden Club has its annual fundraiser this weekend, so she's all in a tizzy, but other than that she's pretty much the same as ever."

"All in a tizzy" was a pretty accurate description of Lindy on a normal day, but Rachel seemed to have a calmer demeanor.

Meredith led Rachel into her office. She gestured toward the two olive-green chairs opposite her desk, and Rachel took a seat in the one closest to the wall. Meredith sat down on the flowered couch.

"This place is beautiful," Rachel said, setting her purse down on the floor. "I love that fireplace, and that old trumpet is gorgeous."

"Thank you." Meredith had worked hard to make the office feel homey and welcoming when Ron had been alive, and now that she and Julia ran the agency, she'd added a few more feminine touches, including an antique trumpet on the mantel. "This was the music room when this was a house, so I put that there to honor the past."

"My mom is the same way." Rachel smiled. "Thank you for seeing me. I wasn't sure if I should call and make an appointment, but Mom said I should just come in and talk to you, so…"

"I'm glad you're here." Meredith was growing curious about what this was all about. "So what can we help you with?"

4

"Well…I have kind of a strange thing to ask. I'm not really sure you all do this, but…"

"Don't worry about that. We've heard it all." Meredith heard quiet footsteps in the hall. "Actually, would it be all right if I ask my business partner to come in and hear this too?"

"Of course." Rachel nodded.

"You couldn't keep me away if you tried." Julia was already coming through the doorway. "Not after I heard that intriguing opening."

Rachel laughed while Julia settled into the other wingback chair.

"So, I just bought a property out by Ebenezer Creek," Rachel said.

"Oh wow." Meredith was familiar with the area, about twenty-five miles north of Savannah. It was rural, swampy—and notable mostly for an incident in which hundreds of enslaved black people had escaped but were drowned in the creek during the Civil War.

"I want to build a small hotel and run ecotours of the swamp from it. Kayaks, mostly, paddling tours, that kind of thing."

"Ooh. That sounds really intriguing," Julia said.

It sounded like a good way to get eaten alive by mosquitoes to Meredith.

"I found a beautiful piece of land adjacent to the creek, and my lawyer has checked it out. It's owned by Effingham County, and they were anxious to get rid of it, so I was able to get it for a song," Rachel said. "It's beautiful too. It's pretty much exactly what I was looking for."

"What's the catch?" There had to be one, Meredith knew, or Rachel wouldn't be sitting here now.

"Well…" Rachel let out a sigh. "There's a house on the property now. It's stood empty for the last thirty years or so."

Meredith didn't even want to imagine the state of that building. The humid summers had probably turned it almost entirely to rot.

"It's a teardown at this point," Rachel said. "That's not the issue. The problem is that…well, don't laugh when I say this. I know it sounds crazy. But apparently there are rumors that the place is haunted, which is probably why the county wasn't able to unload it all those years."

"A haunted house?" Now that was interesting. Meredith loved old homes, and there were plenty of places in Savannah that were rumored to have ghosts that walked the halls.

"I know it's all nonsense. I don't believe in ghosts," Rachel said. Julia was nodding in agreement. "But I know there are plenty of people who might be put off by that kind of thing, and I don't want to risk losing potential customers because of a silly rumor about ghosts."

"You never know. You might get people who book a room in hopes of seeing a ghost," Meredith said. There were several hotels in the Savannah area that kept their rooms full by playing up the rumored ghostly sightings on their property.

"It's not really the vibe I'm going for," Rachel said. "I don't know how much ecotourists and ghost enthusiasts overlap."

"You're probably right," Meredith said with a sigh. Ecotourists cared about sustainability and conserving the land, not unexplained paranormal phenomenon.

"So how can we help?" Julia asked. "We're not exactly ghost hunters."

"Well, my mom's idea was that I might be able to hire you guys to come out and verify that the place is ghost-free, and that would hopefully put the rumors to bed once and for all."

"I see." Meredith was definitely interested, and she could see that Julia was too. "And when were you hoping to have us come out and look at the property?"

"Well…" Rachel let out a nervous laugh. "Demolition is set to begin early next week. So, you know, the sooner the better?"

"So you'd want us to come out in the next day or so?"

Rachel nodded sheepishly.

Meredith looked at Julia, who nodded, and then Meredith explained their rate and fee structure. They told Rachel they would discuss whether they could take the case and let her know as soon as possible.

"Thank you so much," Rachel said, and stood. "I really appreciate your even considering it. I know it's not the kind of case you typically handle."

Meredith walked her out, asking her to give Lindy her best, and then returned to find Julia looking at her calendar on her phone.

"What do you think?" Meredith asked, lowering herself into her desk chair.

"It seems like easy money to me." Julia looked up from her phone. "I have to be back to tail Isabella when she gets done with her tennis lessons, but I'm free this afternoon to go out and see the house if we leave soon."

"Don't you think it seems a little…well, unfair?" Meredith asked. "To charge her for something like this?"

"Why? She needs someone to certify the property ghost-free, and we can figure out a way to provide that service. What's wrong with that?"

Meredith thought about it. "I guess we could check it out," she finally said. She still wasn't sure she felt comfortable charging Rachel anything. "Could we give her a special rate?"

"It's a decent drive from here. We'll need to account for gas and time away from the office."

Julia must have seen how conflicted Meredith felt, because she added, "But sure. This should be a simple task, so maybe we could knock a percentage off the hourly rate?"

Meredith nodded. "That makes sense to me. I'll call her and tell her."

"I have to do more surveillance on Isabella tomorrow, so if we don't go out to see it this afternoon, it will have to wait until Wednesday at the earliest."

Meredith couldn't think of any appointments she had that day, but she turned and pulled up the calendar on her computer and checked it.

"I suppose it would be a nice break from the insurance fraud investigation," she said. She didn't have any meetings she had to attend today. Plus, it was a beautiful day. It would be nice to get out of the office. "I'll see if today works for her," Meredith said, and called the cell phone number Rachel had given her.

"Is there any chance you can show us the property this afternoon?" she asked when Rachel picked up.

"That was quick," Rachel said. "And yes, this afternoon would be great."

"Wonderful." Meredith gave Julia a thumbs-up and wrote down the directions Rachel gave her. "Have your GPS route you to Journeyman's Road. That's the nearest street it will recognize. Then drive past that and onto the dirt road that runs behind it. It's kind of a rough road, and overgrown."

"We'll manage."

"Great," Rachel said. "So you follow that dirt road maybe a mile or so. You'll pass a cemetery, and then you'll go around the bend and you'll see the house. There's an area just in front of the house where it's cleared out a bit, and you can park. I have to run over and talk to my lawyer now, but I could meet you there at, say, noon?"

It was a little past ten now. That would give them time to grab something for lunch and then drive out. "That sounds perfect."

"Wonderful. I really appreciate it. I'll see you there."

"We're meeting her at noon," Meredith said, hanging up the phone.

"I heard that. And did I also hear something about a cemetery?"

"Yes. She said the property is just past a cemetery."

"That won't help with the rumors about the house being haunted," Julia said.

"I guess we'll have to see."

An hour later, they said goodbye to Carmen as they headed out the door. They climbed into Meredith's SUV, and Julia pulled up the GPS app on her phone.

"We'll be a bit early, but maybe we can look around before she gets there," Meredith said.

As she navigated the narrow streets of the historic district, Meredith was pleased to see so many people outside enjoying the beautiful day. The trees, still clad in their lush summer glory, arched over the brick townhomes, and dahlias and cockscombs were blooming in the parks and yards. Once the women got out of the historic area, the streets widened, and they took Route 21 past the shopping centers and gas stations and out of town. They talked about the weekend in the Outer Banks Julia had planned for Beau's upcoming birthday, and then about an antique steamer trunk Beau found at a local estate sale and was refinishing. The buildings gave way to thick stands of tupelo and sweetgum trees draped in Spanish moss, and the larger estates on the outskirts of town turned into smaller shotgun houses and trailers.

"This place already feels like a whole different world," Julia said.

"I wonder if people will really want to come out here to stay in an eco-hotel," Meredith said.

"If it's done up nicely, I imagine they will," Julia said as the turn-off approached. "It sounds nice to me. I bet it's quiet out there."

"So, when we get there, what's our strategy for declaring the place officially not haunted?" Meredith asked. "I suppose we'll need to give it a thorough walk-through, but what kinds of things should we be looking to gather as proof?"

"I have no idea," Julia said. "Maybe we just call out, 'Come out, come out wherever you are'? And then when we don't find any ghosts, we tell Rachel she's in the clear?"

"It seems like there should be something more official than that. But I have no idea what it would be." Meredith turned off onto a smaller road lined with open fields, dotted with small cabins here and there.

"Want me to google 'how to find ghosts'?"

"I don't think we'd want to see the kind of stuff a search like that would bring up." If she was being honest, Meredith could almost see the appeal of believing in ghosts. It would be nice to think that Ron was still around somewhere, watching her, just out of sight. But she didn't believe it. She knew the Bible better than that, and her hope was in something far greater than glimpses of Ron's aura or whatever ghosts were supposed to represent. She trusted that God was faithful and that she would see Ron again someday. Until then, she would just have to be patient.

"I guess we could ask around," Julia said. "And find out why there are rumors to begin with, and hear what people say. Maybe something bad happened out on that property, and that's what's causing the rumors."

"Right," Meredith said. "Something other than all those people drowning, you mean." You couldn't ignore the history of a place, Meredith knew. What had happened on that land was a part of it.

"Wait. Who drowned?" Julia turned her head.

"The slaves who died at Ebenezer Creek. During the Civil War."

"It sounds familiar." Julia turned toward Meredith. "Refresh my memory."

Meredith had been the president of the Savannah Historical Society, and she loved talking about the region's history. She sat up a bit straighter and adjusted her seat belt.

"It was during General Sherman's march to the sea. He'd torched Atlanta and was leading the Union army toward the Port of Savannah."

"I remember that bit. I saw *Gone with the Wind*. Melanie had to give birth in the midst of all that." Julia picked up the Diet Dr Pepper that sat in the cup holder and took a sip.

Meredith stifled a smile. She was glad when people learned the nation's history, no matter how they had come to it.

"Anyway. Sherman. What happened?" Julia put the soda can back into the cup holder.

"As the Northern army marched through Georgia, the Union XIV Corps under Brigadier General Jefferson Davis—"

"The Confederate president?" Julia sounded incredulous.

Meredith shook her head. "That was Jefferson Finis Davis. This Davis, Jefferson C. Davis, fought for the North and was leading thousands of Union soldiers toward Savannah, and hundreds of enslaved people who had fled attached themselves to the group. Davis didn't mind, as long as they were willing to go ahead of his army and smooth out roads so his men could drag their canons over level ground. But as their numbers grew, with women and children, the extra people started to slow down the army and there weren't enough resources to go around. And it didn't help that the Confederate army was following them."

"Oh dear. I can already see this isn't going to end well."

"When they got to Ebenezer Creek, Davis's men built a pontoon bridge so the Union soldiers could go across and press on toward the east and Savannah. The slaves were told to wait on the western side while the army went across first."

"Oh no. Tell me they didn't—"

"That's right. As soon as the last of the Union soldiers crossed the bridge, Davis's men destroyed it, stranding the entire group of men, women, and children on the western side with the Confederate army closing in."

"That's awful."

"The people panicked, and many ran toward the water, afraid of being left behind. Hundreds were drowned or crushed in the ensuing stampede. Those who survived were caught and forced to return to slavery."

"Oh my goodness. That's terrible." Julia shook her head.

"It's one of the more shameful moments in Georgia's history," Meredith said sadly.

"Why don't I know about it?" Julia asked. "It seems like something that should be in all the history books."

Meredith shrugged. "I know a monument was finally erected to mark the spot a while back, but it took a lot of doing. Volunteers gathered petitions for decades before someone finally paid attention. I suppose we all like to hear about the good parts of our history—how the practice of slavery was finally abolished—but no one really wants to remember the awful things that happened along the way."

Julia didn't say anything for a moment. Meredith suspected she was mulling it over in her head.

"Well, if we're looking for ghosts, that story would fit the bill," Julia finally said. "The ghosts of the people drowned by the Union Army."

"There won't be any, of course," Meredith added. "But yes, it seems likely that's why people think the place is haunted. Our job is to look for ways to prove there are no ghosts on the property."

Julia nodded. "Or maybe there was something more recent. We can ask Rachel what she knows, and ask around to see what the neighbors say."

Meredith slowed just after Journeyman's Road, the last spot their GPS recognized, exactly as Rachel had predicted. She turned right onto the unmarked road and kept driving to a gate that stood open. There the pavement turned to dirt, and she slowed down. The dirt path ran along the edge of a swampy creek, with giant tupelo and cypress trees growing in the murky, green-skinned water. Parrot feather, pennywort, and mosquito fern grew in abundance, and Spanish moss draped from the trees. Meredith had seen plenty of striking landscapes throughout the South, but this swamp felt almost primordial.

"Wow," Julia breathed, shaking her head. The canopy of trees cast the area in shadow, but patches of sunlight shone through, dappling the water and the dirt road with golden light. "It's really stunning, isn't it?"

"It's incredible." Meredith was starting to understand what Rachel was envisioning now. She could imagine people coming to visit this distinctive landscape and paddle a canoe through the otherworldly swamp. "Look, there's the graveyard."

Up ahead to the left was a cleared area with moss-covered headstones circled by a stone fence.

"What an odd place for a cemetery. There's no church or anything nearby," Julia said.

"It could be a family graveyard," Meredith said. Those weren't uncommon in this area—in generations past, a section of a family's land would be set aside as a burial ground for members of the family.

"Must be," Julia said. The road grew bumpier and the brush more overgrown, but finally they saw a tall white structure through the trees.

"That must be the house," Meredith said. As they drew closer, she saw that it had once been a grand plantation-style home, with a columned front porch and evenly spaced windows on the two floors. But now the windows on the first floor were boarded up, shutters were hanging loose, vines snaked up the facade of the house, and a portion of the roof on the second floor had collapsed.

"What a shame," Meredith said, taking in the decayed grandeur of the place. "It must have been gorgeous once."

"It's creepy," Julia said flatly. "I might have to reconsider my theory about ghosts." She unbuckled her seat belt as Meredith parked in a cleared space under a stand of oak and sweetgum trees, next to a blue hatchback.

"Rachel must be here already," Meredith said, stepping out of the car. She took a deep breath and looked around as she shut the door behind her. She had the sense that nature was in the process of reclaiming this whole place.

"Hi there." Meredith turned. Rachel came around the side of the house. "You found it."

"It is tucked out of the way, isn't it?" Julia said. "But it's a beautiful piece of land."

"And what a gorgeous old home," Meredith said. "At least, it must have been at one time."

"Yes, it clearly was beautiful once," Rachel said. "It's too bad it's fallen into such decay. Once the county took over the land, they locked it up tight, and no one really took care of it. This is what happens after thirty years of neglect." She gestured toward the decrepit porch.

"You said you're planning to tear it down?" Meredith was usually adamant about restoring old homes instead of knocking them down, and her years at the historical society had only reinforced that inclination, but even she wasn't sure this house could be saved.

"I don't think it's structurally sound at this point," Rachel said. "Unfortunately, I think it has to go."

Meredith nodded. "Is there anything you can salvage from the inside?"

"I haven't checked," Rachel said. "I've been kind of afraid to go inside."

"Wait. What?" Julia had been walking toward the house, but she stopped and turned back. "You bought this place, and you haven't even been inside yet?"

"It's really more the land I was interested in," Rachel said. "Did you all see that creek on the way in? Isn't it something?"

"It is stunning yet sad and eerie at the same time," Meredith confirmed. "But Julia's right. You can't tear this place down without at least looking inside the house. Who knows what kind of treasures are inside?"

"Or what kinds of vermin and rodents," Rachel said nervously.

Julia was looking at Meredith, who caught her eye and nodded.

"We have to be able to tell people that we've looked the place over thoroughly if we want them to believe us when we say there are no ghosts here," Meredith said as authoritatively as she could. She was dying to see what was inside. She glanced at the front door, which was boarded over and chained shut, locked with a padlock.

"Do you have a key?" Julia asked, already marching up the sagging porch steps.

"They gave me one at the closing," Rachel said. "It's here. But still, it's boarded shut."

"Careful," Meredith called to Julia, but the old wooden boards held her weight. Julia put her hand on one of the boards that nailed the front door shut and yanked on it. "It's totally rotted," she called, and yanked a few more times until the board came away in her hands. She did the same with the second board. "Where's that key?"

Rachel fumbled with her key ring and eventually found a brass key. She held it out to Meredith, who carried it up the spongy porch steps, which creaked and groaned under her feet, and handed it to Julia. Julia fitted it into the padlock, turned it, and, after struggling with it for a few minutes, the lock popped open.

Meredith helped Julia pull away the remaining boards, and the front door swung open when she pushed on it. Julia stepped in first.

"Oh my goodness," Julia called. "You guys have to see this."

"What is it?" The way she said it made Meredith's heart race.

"I can't even—I don't—just look."

Meredith didn't hesitate. Was it an animal? Was there some gruesome scene inside the home? Was it dangerous? She stepped inside, and Rachel followed just behind.

Meredith's breath left her lungs. Whatever she had been expecting, it wasn't this. The smell was powerful, but she couldn't identify it. She looked around and took it all in. "Oh my."

"What do you think happened here?" Julia asked, her voice shaky.

Meredith shook her head. "I have no idea."

Chapter Two

MEREDITH COULDN'T MAKE SENSE OF it. She stepped into the once-grand entry hall of the crumbling house and looked around. A wide staircase rose to the second floor, the carpeted steps thick with dust. The walls were lined with a baby blue brocade wallpaper, now peeling off in strips and spotted with mildew. Cobwebs hung in long strings from the brass chandelier. The whole place had the smell of damp and decay.

But Meredith had expected all this. The house had stood empty for thirty years. It was what she saw in the room that branched off to the left that confused her.

"That must have been the dining room," Julia said, stepping toward the space. Meredith followed a step behind, trailed by Rachel. A long oval table made of what must have once been polished walnut, now dulled and warped, was surrounded by ten matching chairs, their padded seats moldering. The walls were lined with the same blue wallpaper, and the heavy drapery, turned a muddy brown by damp and dust, hung beside the broken windows. A china cabinet stood in the corner, the glass front intact, the plates and cups and glasses lined up in neat rows, now gray with a dusty film.

"What in the world?" Rachel asked, stepping around Meredith for a better look.

Meredith also stepped closer. On the table, there were two place settings down toward the far end. One held the remains of a meal, long rotted and covered with many different kinds of fungus. Next to that, there was a setting of silverware, with no plate but a glass lined with a brownish film, and there was a newspaper spread wide open. An orange juice container with a mug next to it held an impressive quantity of various kinds of mold.

Julia was already pulling latex gloves out of her purse, and she handed a pair to Meredith and one to Rachel. They often had such things with them, since you never knew what might happen on a job. Then Meredith walked to the end of the table and examined the place settings.

"It looks like they were in the middle of a meal," Julia said, shaking her head.

Meredith thought the same thing. Had the people who lived here just up and left in the middle of breakfast? She lifted the corner of the newspaper and squinted. The ink had faded, but she saw that it was from September 6, 1988. A cosmonaut spacecraft had landed safely with two astronauts on board, according to the headline. Meredith pulled out her phone and took several pictures of the scene.

Julia turned and started through the doorway that led to the next room. Meredith followed a step behind, and she found herself in the kitchen. The wooden cabinets had once been white, and the hardware had a distinctly midcentury look. But it was the sink that drew her eye—it was piled with dishes. Dirty glasses lined the butcher-block counter, and there was a pot on the stove filled with what must once have been some kind of food. A thick layer of dust coated everything. A white refrigerator stood at the end of the row of cabinets along the southern wall. As Julia moved toward it, Meredith braced herself for the smell. When they'd lost power during a storm a few years back, everything in their fridge had gone bad. There was no telling what was inside this thing after all these years.

Julia opened it long enough for them to see that it was filled with half-empty ketchup bottles, yogurt containers, a jug of milk, and other unidentifiables. There was no light and no refrigeration.

"Close it, quick," Rachel said, her hand in front of her nose.

Julia shoved it closed, and they all wrinkled their noses and moved away from the rancid smell.

"It's like they just up and left in the middle of a meal and never came back," Meredith said. She tried to make sense of it, and she couldn't. There was a small wooden table in the corner there, and it was piled with books and magazines as well as all sorts of odds and ends. Meredith took photos of this room as well.

"It's very strange," Julia confirmed. "But—oh. Wow."

"What?"

Meredith moved over and saw that Julia had walked out of the kitchen toward what looked like it had once been a sunroom at the back of the house. The glass was boarded up, but somehow vines had snaked their way inside a couple of panes of broken glass, intertwining with the white wicker furniture. The door that led out the back of the house was also boarded shut. Beyond that, there was a hallway that no doubt led to some sort of living room, but most of the hallway was blocked by a couch lying on its end. It was nearly long enough to touch the ceiling and upholstered in heavy red velvet, with an elaborately carved dark wood frame.

"What is that doing here?" Rachel asked. Meredith shook her head, but as she stepped closer, she realized the reason.

"There's a door there," she said, pointing at the white trim around the small section of wood that she made out. "What do you think, a basement?"

"Has to be," Rachel said quietly.

"Why would you push a couch up to block the door to the basement?" Julia asked.

For the first time since they'd entered the house, Meredith felt a prickle of fear. She could think of a number of reasons you would block the basement door with a couch and abandon a house, and none of them were good.

"Does it smell like smoke?" Rachel asked.

Meredith sniffed. She did catch the faint odor of smoke up close to this door. "Vaguely."

"I smell it too," Julia said. "But it's not very strong."

"Maybe someone is burning leaves nearby?" Rachel suggested. Meredith wasn't sure what to think.

"Let's leave that for now," Meredith said, and squeezed her way past the couch, arching away so she didn't brush against it, and found a small powder room to one side, a living room, and what must have once been a formal parlor.

While Julia went to look into the parlor, Meredith walked into the living room, carpeted in a thick brown pile. An enormous big-screen TV console stood in the corner, its fake walnut veneer peeling. She hadn't seen one of those things in years. A smaller couch that matched the one pushed up against the door and a brown leather recliner filled the space. Everything was covered in a thick layer of dust. No one had been inside the house in a very long time, that was clear. A stack of magazines sat on a side table, the top one open to an article about a miraculous rescue. It was almost as if someone had gotten up in the middle of reading the story, meaning to come back and finish it.

"It's more of the same in here," Julia called from the parlor. "Except that this room has had a lot of water damage."

Meredith poked her head inside to see that this furniture had once been nice antiques, but several of the chairs were rotting and the upholstery had molded. There were spots of mold streaking the walls. Meredith remembered that part of the roof had caved in, and realized that this room must be underneath that section. But there was a book lying spine up on one of the chairs. Meredith craned her neck. The book was *Jane Eyre*. Had someone intended to come back and keep reading?

"It's almost like they went out for a minute and didn't come back," Meredith said.

Instead of responding, Julia turned and stepped into the hallway and headed for the main staircase.

"Do you think you should—" Meredith started, but Julia was already saying, "These are sturdy. Solid oak, if I guess right. These things will stand forever."

Meredith looked at Rachel, who shrugged, and they both started to follow Julia up the steps. The runner that went up them was stained gray and let out a funky odor with each step. The hallway branched off in both directions at the top of the stairs. Julia turned to the right, and Meredith and Rachel followed behind her.

"Look at this," Julia said, stepping into the first bedroom. It must have belonged to a young woman, Meredith saw, as it had a lavender quilted bedspread balled up at the end of the bed and several faded photographs lined along the bottom of the mirror over the vanity table. A piece of pink fabric was draped over the chair in front. Julia walked over and lifted it, and the fabric fell into the shape of a dress with puff sleeves and a sweetheart neckline. It was covered in dust, and the magenta fabric was faded in the spots where the sunlight had hit it for years.

"Does it *get* more eighties?" Rachel asked.

"It's like she took it off and never got around to hanging it up," Meredith said.

They moved down the hall, toward what must have once been the master bedroom, Meredith supposed. It contained a queen-sized bed, though the covers had been shoved to the floor at some point. They walked inside and while Julia went over to look at the dresser and Rachel studied a group of framed photos on a small bookshelf, Meredith moved toward the bedside table on the closer side of the bed. A Bible, swollen with moisture, sat on top.

The room was dim, the windows surrounded by overgrown trees, so Meredith turned on the flashlight on her phone and opened the cover and saw the name DAISY BUFORD written on the first page. ON THE OCCASION OF YOUR WEDDING, JUNE 7, 1966, someone had written in neat black cursive. She picked the Bible up and flipped through the warped pages, and she saw that Daisy had underlined many favorite verses and had written notes on the margins throughout. She had underlined and starred Micah 6:8: "He has shown you, O mortal, what is good. And what does the LORD require of you? To act justly and to love mercy and to walk humbly with your God." Meredith had always loved that verse.

She took a photo of that page before she set the Bible down gently and reached for the handle on the nightstand's drawer. The wood was warped, and it stuck, but she jiggled it, and the drawer slid out. Inside, there were a few childish drawings and a handful of photographs of young children, but what caught her eye was a stack of envelopes bound with a rubber band. She pulled out the envelopes, and she saw that they were letters written with a shaky hand on yellowed notebook paper.

"Look at this."

Meredith turned and saw that Julia was holding out a man's wallet made of brown leather. "It was in the top drawer of the dresser, just sitting there with his other things."

"Is there anything inside?" Meredith still held the letters as she crossed the floor to get a closer look. She saw that the wallet had been tucked into an underwear and sock drawer.

"Yes." Julia shook her head. "Most notably, a driver's license. No cash, though."

"A license?" Rachel had come over to see as well. "Whose?"

"Earl Walter Buford," Julia said, squinting at the small print. "Born February 17, 1945. Home address, 25 Ebenezer Road."

Meredith and Rachel both leaned in to get a better look. The photo showed a solidly built man with brown hair surrounding a bald spot.

"Why would he leave this here?" Meredith asked.

"Hang on. There's something else here too," Julia said, and pulled out a folded scrap of paper that had been tucked behind the license.

Meredith leaned forward and tried to make out the scrawled letters.

Bring the cash to Mario's by midnight Saturday. He'll be waiting.

"What could that mean?" Meredith leaned back.

Julia sighed. "Honestly, it's pretty clear. We just don't know who wrote it or why."

Meredith didn't have an answer. She wanted to take a picture, but she needed both hands, so she slipped the stack of letters into her purse and then snapped a photo. She pointed to the Bible on the nightstand. "That Bible was owned by a Daisy Buford. She must have been married to Earl."

"And I think they had six kids," Rachel said. She gestured toward the bookshelf. "There are family photos over there."

Meredith and Julia both followed her to the bookshelf and leaned in to see the pictures. There was a formal black-and-white wedding portrait of what had to be Daisy and a much-younger Earl. Daisy wore a simple floor-length dress and lacy veil as they stood at the front of an ornate church. Beside that was a studio portrait of six children. The oldest, a boy, couldn't have been more than twelve, and the youngest was probably less than a year. Three boys and three girls, one of whom had striking red hair, Meredith noted. The clothing and hairstyles dated this to the midseventies. Meredith took photos of each of the pictures.

"Good thing they had this big house," Julia said, shaking her head. But where were those children now?

They moved out of the master bedroom and went into a few more bedrooms, all in various states of decay, but each left mostly intact, as before. They didn't enter the bedroom at the far end of the hallway, where a tree limb had crashed through the roof at some point. Kudzu vines had found their way in through the hole and were entwined around the furniture and crawled up the walls. The floor leading toward the room was spongy, and the smells of rotting wood and decaying matter were strong.

Meredith took lots of photos, and then the women trooped back down the stairs and out the creaking front door and gathered on the front porch. The air smelled fresh and clean after the dank interior.

"It's almost like the whole family just vanished one day," Meredith said, shaking her head.

"But where did they go? And why?" Julia added.

Meredith didn't know. But none of the possibilities that came to mind were good.

"Is it possible they just, I don't know, moved on?" Rachel asked. But even as she said it, Meredith could hear the doubt in her voice.

"I don't think so," Meredith said, thinking about that Bible, those family photos, the stack of letters tucked into the nightstand. She realized she still had them in her pocket. Well, she wasn't going back in there to return them now. "Why would they leave all their treasures behind? I didn't see much of great material value in there, but they left behind a lot of things with serious sentimental value."

Julia was nodding. "But what's the alternative? That the family just...*vanished*?"

Meredith didn't have an answer.

"Maybe whatever's in that blocked-off basement will explain it," Rachel said.

Goodness. Meredith had almost forgotten about that basement. "Should we try to move the couch and see what's down there?"

"I think we have to." Julia was already heading back inside. Rachel and Meredith followed behind, and they shoved and pushed, but they couldn't budge it.

"What in the world? How can this thing be so heavy?" Meredith asked. She and Julia were no spring chickens, but Rachel was in good shape, and the three of them should have been able to move it. But, defeated, they returned to the porch once more, and then followed Julia around to the side of the house, where she pointed out cellar doors that had also been nailed shut, before they returned to the yard.

"Well, one thing is clear," Meredith said. "If I believed in ghosts, this would be a prime location to find them."

Rachel laughed nervously.

"She's joking," Julia said. "Neither of us actually believes in ghosts. So I think it's safe to say that we can certify this house ghost-free."

"Yes, but now I'm not going to be able to get this family out of my head," Meredith said. "I know I'm going to keep thinking about them and wondering what happened to them to make them up and vanish, leaving their family treasures behind."

"I'm really curious now too," Rachel said.

"Which is why we're also going to find out what happened to them," Julia said, as if reading Meredith's mind.

"You'd better believe we are."

Chapter Three

Willie,

I didn't want you to find out this way. For something like this... well, I've tried calling your house over and over again, but Eldan says you're not there every time. He won't tell me where you are or where I can find you. I don't know if you're there hiding out or if you're really gone, but I finally decided that I needed to find you and tell you what's going on because I can't make a decision like this without talking to you first.

I'm pregnant, Willie. It's yours, of course. And I don't know what to do. I am so scared.

Please come by. Daddy hasn't been around much so you don't need to worry about him.

—R

Back in the car, Julia was making notes on a yellow legal pad while Meredith drove back down the rutted dirt road.

"They had to be in serious trouble." Julia tapped her pen against the notepad. "To just up and go off like that, leaving everything behind."

"I agree," Meredith said. "But what kind of trouble? That's what we need to figure out."

They drove back past the cemetery, and Meredith wished they could stop and take a peek, but they had to get back. They had stayed at the house much longer than either of them had anticipated, and Julia needed to do surveillance on the cheating wife at four. Under different circumstances, she might have simply put a tracking device on the wife's car and monitored her remotely. But that wasn't *technically* legal, and their client needed evidence that would hold up in court, so Julia was stuck with traditional boots-on-the-ground surveillance.

"There was that note in Earl's wallet," Julia said. She set the pen down in the console and picked up Meredith's phone, which sat in the cup holder. She pulled up the photo and read from the screen to make sure she was remembering it right. "'Bring the money to Mario's by midnight Saturday. He'll be waiting.'"

"Sounds like blackmail to me," Meredith said. "So maybe someone had some information the Bufords really didn't want to get out, and instead of paying up, they just left."

"It's something we could look into," Julia said. "We'll need to find out who Mario is and try to figure out who wrote this note."

"And what Earl was being blackmailed for," Meredith said. "It must have been pretty bad for them not to take anything with them when they left."

Julia picked her pen up again and tapped it against the legal pad. "Why wouldn't Earl at least take his wallet when he left? Wouldn't he need his ID?"

"Witness protection program?" Meredith suggested. "Maybe he didn't need his ID because the government was giving him a new one."

"I suppose it's possible," Julia said.

But in Meredith's heart, it didn't feel right. "You don't just vanish in the middle of breakfast for the witness protection program, do you? Surely they let you finish your orange juice before you start your new life?"

"I have no idea," Julia said. "It's not something that comes up a lot in real court cases, as much as it seems like it in books, so it's not something I have any real experience with."

Meredith braked as the groove at the end of the drive approached, and after the car dipped down, they were back on smooth pavement again.

"Maybe it was a sickness." Meredith suggested. "A fast-moving swamp virus that took them all before anyone had a chance to call for help?"

"Let's hope not." Julia shuddered.

"It's an awful thought, but better than the alternative, if we're contemplating death as a cause for the house to be abandoned," Meredith said. "There could be a different reason they all died suddenly."

"You think they were murdered?" Julia's eyes widened.

"I have no way of knowing. It's just a suggestion." She shrugged. "It would explain why they all vanished like that."

"And why no one wanted the property afterward, I suppose," Julia added.

"And it could help explain the rumors about the place being haunted," Meredith said. "An entire family being murdered would be enough to start some rumors."

Silence filled the vehicle for a moment while Meredith contemplated that grisly possibility.

"But there was no blood," Julia pointed out.

"There's always the basement," Meredith said. Even as the words came out of her mouth, a chill went down her spine. Could that have been why the couch had been pushed up to block the basement door? To hide a gruesome scene? "Or maybe they weren't killed in the house. It could have been anywhere. Or maybe something entirely different happened."

"There's so much we don't know," Julia said with a sigh. "We're just guessing at this point."

"You're right," Meredith said. "I suppose the first thing to do is to see whether there were any murders in the area around the time the place was abandoned."

"Speaking of which, we should probably try to find out exactly *when* the place was abandoned," Julia said. "The newspaper said 1988, and judging by the furniture and clothes inside, that seems about right, but it would be nice to know for sure."

"I bet we could get information about that at the courthouse," Meredith said. "That's probably our best bet to find information about when Effingham County took over the property, as well as vital records for the family."

"Death certificates, you mean," Julia said.

"Or birth, or marriage, or whatever," Meredith added. "There appear to have been several children. Maybe we could find their names and see if any of them are still out there somewhere."

"That's a good strategy," Julia said. "I wish we could go there now, but I'm already going to be cutting it close."

"Maybe I can go tomorrow, while you're surveilling Isabella." Meredith said. The Effingham County courthouse would be in Springfield, which was not too far from where they were now.

"Good idea. And then maybe on Wednesday we can go back to the house."

"What? Why?"

"We need to get into the basement, for one thing."

The thought filled Meredith with a sense of raw, unfiltered dread. "Do we really have to?"

"Of course we do. There might be some important clue down there."

"Like their skeletons," Meredith said, suddenly queasy.

"Possibly, but probably more mundane than that," Julia said. "But we'll never know if we can't get that couch moved." She sighed. "I wish we could go back tomorrow, but I promised Dennis that I'd tail his wife to her tennis lessons and lunch tomorrow."

"I'll start at the courthouse and see what I can find," Meredith said. She was used to digging through records. "We'll find out what happened to that family."

***

After they got back to Savannah and Julia had gone off to run surveillance on Isabella, Meredith tried to focus on the insurance fraud case. A thirtysomething man named Aaron Whitaker had claimed he'd been injured in a fall off a ladder at his job at a large roofing company, and he had been claiming workers' comp while he healed for the past four months. The man's employer and the insurance company had doubts about the severity of his injury and whether he was actually still unable to work, and the insurance company had hired Magnolia Investigations to find out whether he was truly badly injured.

Meredith spent some time looking over the medical codes that his doctor had billed, and she had no way to know if they were legitimate. She needed to get out and watch him and see if he was actually as badly injured as he claimed. She decided it was time for some field work, so she googled him to make sure she knew what he looked like—a big guy with close-cropped brown hair and a tattoo of an anchor on his forearm, from his navy days, no doubt. From his file, she knew that he'd served eight years of active duty and that he was divorced, with a young daughter he saw every other weekend.

Meredith looked up his address, said goodbye to Carmen, and drove to the western part of town, where Aaron Whitaker lived. She parked in front of his home on Wayne Street. A car was in the drive-way, a large black SUV, but there were no lights or sounds coming from inside the home.

Meredith looked around. There was a woman tending to her rosebushes in front of the house next door. Meredith strode over and put on her best Junior League smile.

"My, those are beautiful roses. Are they Boscobels?"

The woman turned and nodded. "You have a good eye." She was probably ten or fifteen years older than Meredith, with white hair and a floppy wide-brimmed hat.

"They're gorgeous. I've never seen them that pink."

"The secret is in the soil. I compost in the back." The woman gestured toward the rear of the house. "So much better than commercial soil."

"Well, it works." Meredith put on her best innocent smile. "I was trying to get in touch with your neighbor Aaron. Is there any chance you know where he is?"

"I'm afraid not. I'm not sure what he's up to these days. He's around a lot more, but he seems to come and go at all hours." She used clippers to deadhead a withered rose. "Is he in trouble?" She seemed just a bit too excited about that idea, Meredith thought.

"Oh, no. I just have a few questions to ask him." Meredith hoped that would satisfy her. "It's about his job," she added, after the woman gave her a quizzical look.

"Oh. Well, he's been around so much I figured he didn't have one anymore."

This was exactly the kind of neighbor Meredith liked in her line of work—she noticed everything.

"So his schedule has changed?" Meredith asked.

"Oh yes. He used to do construction, and now he never seems to leave the house during the day."

Well, that could mean he very well was injured, and resting his back.

"But he goes out every evening," the woman added.

"Interesting. Do you know where he goes?" She tried to keep her voice from sounding too interested.

"I couldn't say."

She couldn't say? Or she wouldn't?

"Does he drive when he goes out?" Meredith pressed her.

"He usually walks. Safer that way." She clipped away more dead buds.

"Safer? What do you mean?"

"When you've had a few, you know?"

"Oh. So he goes out to a…bar? Or a nightclub?"

"Well, like I said, I couldn't say for sure. But a lot of the men around here work in construction, like that sweet Nestor on the corner. He brings me tamales every Christmas and checks on me during storms. He tells me that a lot of the construction guys gather at Jimmy's after work."

Jimmy's. She assumed the place couldn't be that hard to find.

"Has his daughter been around?"

"I've seen her a few times."

"Have you seen him playing with her, riding bikes or anything like that?"

"She rides her bike sometimes, but he stays in the house."

"In the past few weeks, have you seen Aaron doing anything active? Jogging, playing basketball, lifting anything heavy? Mowing his lawn?"

The woman snorted. "Not likely. But then, that's not any different from normal."

"He's not very active normally?"

"Look at the state of that yard." She clucked her tongue. "I think not."

Meredith considered this. It was overgrown, for sure, and not well tended. Was that because Aaron was unable to do yard work? Or just that he didn't enjoy it? She needed to find out.

"Have you lived in the neighborhood for a while?"

"Oh yes. Thirty-two years."

"I bet you've seen a lot of change in that time."

"Indeed." The woman went on a rant about the types of people who were moving in and how this area used to be safe, and Meredith took that as her cue to leave.

She thanked the woman, and, once she was back in her car, pulled up Jimmy's on a map. It was just a few blocks away, on the far side of Monterey Square. She might as well take a gander, she decided.

She navigated the narrow streets and parked down the block from it then considered what to do. She could go inside and try to find Aaron, maybe strike up a conversation. But there were a few problems with this. Aside from her general distaste for bars, there was the fact that she was a sixty-five-year-old woman. If she had been in her twenties and could still rock a miniskirt, she might have had a shot, but no young man wanted to talk to a grandma while he was having a drink with his friends. The biggest problem, though, was that she needed to get photographic or video evidence of Aaron doing something that showed he was not really injured, and even if she could get that evidence inside Jimmy's, it wouldn't hold up in court. In the state of Georgia, it was illegal to make a recording inside a private space without the consent of all parties being recorded. Inside a crowded bar, that would be nearly impossible. She would need to catch Aaron either outside, in a public space, or get him to agree to be recorded doing something that proved he was lying. Neither seemed very likely. Still, she could watch and see if he came out now, and see where he went after that.

Meredith sat in her car and tried to work on the crossword puzzles she kept in her purse for just such occasions. She tried to focus on the clues, looking up between each to make sure Aaron hadn't come out of Jimmy's, but her mind kept drifting back to that abandoned house and the faces of those Buford children in that photograph on the dresser. Where had they all gone? Were they out there somewhere?

Meredith remembered the letters she'd tucked into her purse back at the Buford house, and she pulled them out now. She hadn't intended to take these, but now that she had them, she might as well see what they were about.

The envelopes were yellowed, and the rubber band that held them together was so rotted it had split in places. She slid it off gently and picked up the first letter. It was addressed to Willie Buford at 25 Ebenezer Place, and the postmark showed it had been mailed from Springfield on July 2, 1985. There was no return address. She took the page out and unfolded it. It was a letter, written on white binder paper in shaky blue ink.

Willie,

Eldan had told me over and over that you weren't at home, but I needed to see for myself, so I went by the house this afternoon. When I got there, your daddy was chewing out some lady trying to collect signatures on a petition, and he was screaming. I hid in the trees, just like you showed me, until he went out to the river and took the boat and I knew it was safe. Then I came to the door, but Eldan told me you weren't around. He said he didn't know how to find you. Maybe it's

foolish to be writing you since I don't know if you'll ever get this letter, but I am going to mail it anyway. I am keeping the baby. It is due in November. I hope you get this before then.

You know where to find me.

—R

The next letter had been sent a few weeks later.

Willie,

I don't know when you'll get this letter, or if you'll ever get it, but I had to try. I can feel the baby kicking. I know it's a boy, though the doctor says I shouldn't get my hopes up. My daddy didn't want me to waste the money for a doctor, but I met a woman who has been very nice to me. She's the lady I saw your daddy yelling at about that petition. After I left your house that time, she was waiting at the bus stop a mile from your place, and while we were waiting we talked. We were going the same direction too, so we talked more on the bus. She is a kind woman, and she called me that night to check on me and insisted I see her doctor and took me to the clinic. It was free, so my daddy didn't know what he was talking about, again. Anyway, the doctor said the baby is fine. Please call or write to me when you get this.

—R

Meredith scanned the next two in the stack, and they were further pleas for Willie to find her and acknowledge his child. Had Willie ever gotten these letters? She'd have to keep reading to find out. But Daisy Buford had. Daisy had read them, and she'd kept them. In fact, she hadn't just kept them; she'd stored them next to her bed, alongside her children's drawings and photographs. These letters were precious to her. But why? Who was Willie, and what did he have to do with Daisy? Could *she* have been R? But no, even if the initials had matched, the timing didn't work out. Daisy had been married to Earl for nearly twenty years before these letters were written. Was R one of Daisy's children? Or was Willie? But Willie didn't come off looking very good in these letters, nor did Willie's father. Then again, if Willie was one of the older Buford children in that photo on the dresser, he could have been about the right age to become a young father in 1985. And the description of R hiding in the trees until Willie's father went off down the river did make sense at that old house in Ebenezer Creek. It could have happened there, from what she'd seen of the place.

Meredith wasn't sure what to think. All she knew was that these letters might be the saddest of all the sad things they'd found in that house today.

Meredith reached for the next envelope, but then the door of Jimmy's opened and Aaron came out. She recognized his close-cropped hair under an Atlanta Braves cap and the wide forehead she'd seen in his pictures. Meredith watched him walk down the street, back toward his home. She needed to follow him. She set the letters down, and climbed out of her car and walked about twenty feet behind him. She tried to subtly position her phone, set to record, to get a good view in case he... Well, she wasn't quite sure what she thought he might do, she realized, but if he lifted something heavy or broke out in a jog, she would be there to capture it on her camera. She followed behind him as he threaded through Monterey Square and back to the west side of town, and she stayed on the corner as he walked into his yard.

She hadn't caught him doing anything that proved he was cheating his employer's insurance. Not yet anyway. She would keep looking though. For now, she headed back to her car, enjoying the cooler air as the sun slipped behind the trees on this beautiful day.

Once in her car, Meredith checked the time. She had a project she'd planned to start tonight, so she didn't want to stay at work too late. But she had a few things she wanted to take care of, and she decided she could stop in at the office for a bit before heading home.

Julia was out tailing Isabella, but Meredith said hello to Carmen and settled in at her computer. She pulled up a new browser window and typed in the words MURDER EBENEZER CREEK. Several sites that talked about the drowned slaves came up, but there wasn't anything that seemed to suggest a family had been killed in their home. She tried FAMILY MURDER EFFINGHAM COUNTY and several similar terms, but they turned up no useful results.

"I'm going to head out."

Meredith shrieked.

"*Lo siento,*" Carmen said. "I didn't realize you didn't hear me coming down the hallway."

"It's okay," Meredith said. Now that she was breathing again, she felt silly. The floor in this building creaked so loudly it was impossible to sneak up on anyone. How had she not heard Carmen coming toward her? "I must have been more wrapped up in this than I realized."

"What are you researching?" Carmen leaned against the doorframe. She'd put a light jean jacket over her dress and had a messenger bag draped over her shoulder.

"I was trying to find out if a family had been murdered," Meredith admitted sheepishly. "Which probably explains why I was so jumpy."

"Yikes. That's darker than what you usually do."

"Yeah, well, I can't find any evidence that it's true," Meredith said. "So let's hope it's not."

"I second that." Carmen straightened up and saluted Meredith. "I'm taking off, boss."

"Have a good night, Carmen."

"Don't stay here too long," Carmen said in response. "And maybe don't research such dark things when you're here alone either."

"I won't stay for long," Meredith promised. She did need to get going. She wanted to have time to get started on her project. But she had time for just a couple more searches first. She waved goodbye to Carmen and turned back to her computer.

EARL BUFORD MURDER, she tried. And then, when that didn't turn up any results, just EARL BUFORD. She found a few social media profiles for men with similar names but nothing that looked like a link to the man whose wallet they had found that day.

Well, the internet had its limitations; she knew that well enough. If it didn't, she would be out of a job, after all. It would take some real on-the-ground sleuthing to find out more about the Buford family.

Meredith turned off her computer, packed up her purse, and turned off the lights. She used her key to lock the front door, and then she walked down the front steps. She climbed into her car in the small lot at the back of the building and drove the short distance home. There were so many people out this evening, enjoying the cool fresh air and it made Meredith happy to see them after the oppressively hot summer months when everyone stayed inside as much as possible.

She kicked off her shoes when she came in the door and patted GK on the head. He sat mutely by his food dish, looking up at her with hope in his eyes.

"All right, you little beggar," she said, and emptied a can of food into his bowl. The cat dove for the food, as if he was afraid someone else might get to it first, and Meredith laughed and refilled his water dish. She saw that she had missed a call from Quin, a friend she'd first met investigating a case. Sometimes she thought he might become more than a friend, and sometimes she thought Quin felt the same way, but they were taking things slowly. She called him back, and they chatted for a bit. Then she made herself a light dinner—grilled chicken, salad, and green beans—and, once she'd cleaned up the kitchen, she headed upstairs and into the guest bedroom that Ron had used as his workshop.

After Ron had died, dear friends had boxed up his clothing, collections, and items from his home office and stored them in here, where they'd sat all this time. Meredith knew she needed to go through the boxes at some point to figure out what should be tossed, what was worth keeping, and what needed to be passed along to other members of the family. But she'd been waiting until she felt strong enough to be able to handle it. Two years later, she knew enough time would never pass. She would never really be able to reconcile herself to life without him, and that was what going through his things felt like. But she didn't want to it put off any longer. She had promised herself that starting today she would figure out what to do with his things, and she wouldn't get distracted until she was done. She knew there were things Ron had wanted Chase and Carter to have, and it wasn't fair to them to keep this all boxed up any longer.

Meredith flipped on the light switch and the overhead light flicked on, illuminating several sets of Ron's golf clubs and the plastic boxes with his coin collection set against the far wall. There was a wooden table set up in one corner of the room. Ron hadn't been particularly handy, but he had needed a space to assemble the buildings and decorations he'd acquired for his collection of toy trains. The workshop area was still filled with neatly labeled drawers and stacked plastic boxes of various parts and tools. She'd deal with the workshop later; for now, she turned her attention to the plastic bins on the floor. She recognized her friend Mary Ellen's neat handwriting on the labels that read RON'S THINGS. She picked up one of the largest blue plastic boxes, but it was heavier than she expected, and she set it down quickly on the closest surface she could find. It was a bookcase, she saw. Oh, right. She'd forgotten about that. The beautiful glass-fronted barrister bookcase had been in Ron's home office, and he'd intended for Carter to have it. Meredith had always loved the piece, and she would be glad to see it go to their eldest son. It wasn't doing anyone any good down here. She decided to deal with it first.

She pulled her phone from the pocket of her cardigan and found Carter's name and pressed CALL.

"Hi, Mom. What's up?"

She could tell by the faraway sound that he had answered the call on the Bluetooth in his car.

"Hi, honey. How is everything going?"

"It's fine. Just heading home from work. Is everything okay there?"

She hated the long hours Carter worked, especially because that meant Sherri Lynn was probably home feeding the kids dinner on her own. But she knew better than to say that now. She'd made that mistake in the past, and it hadn't gone well.

"Everything is fine here. I'm just in the spare room going through your father's things, and I found this bookcase he wanted you to have."

"Oh right. That's a beautiful piece."

"Well, he intended it to go to you, so I'm wondering if you might be able to come down and get it sometime."

"I'm sure I can, Mom. But are you sure you want to part with it?"

Carter had always had a tender heart, and she'd always appreciated how much he cared about other people's feelings.

"I don't have any place for it anyway, and it would make your father happy if you had it."

"All right. Well, if you're sure, I'll come get it."

She heard the sound of a blinker, and then he continued.

"Actually, I'll be coming to see a client just outside of Savannah for lunch on Wednesday. Is there any chance I could grab it while I'm in town then?"

"That should work just fine." That was sooner than she'd been expecting, but she wasn't about to say no to seeing Carter in two days.

"Perfect. I'll give you a call when I have a better idea of timing."

"That sounds great." Meredith asked about Sherri Lynn and the kids, and they chatted for a moment. Then Carter said he was just pulling into his driveway, and Meredith knew she should let him go so he could focus on spending some time with his wife and kids.

The bookcase was settled then, so she turned to the box she'd set on top. She unlatched the lid, lifted it off gently, and set it aside.

No wonder it had been so heavy. This box was full of books. Inside, she found yellowed paperbacks of the *Aeneid* and the *Odyssey*, as well as thick biographies of presidents and other military heroes. There were several volumes in the Civil War, a perennial topic of interest for Ron. Ron had also been fascinated by the Cold War, so there were several history books about life behind the Iron Curtain, as well as novels about Russian spies. Meredith surveyed the lot. She couldn't imagine any of it having much commercial value. She decided to take pictures and send them to Carter and Chase and let them lay claim if they saw anything that interested them. Otherwise, she'd take them to the thrift store.

She spread the books out and took a picture, then packed the books back up and set the box carefully on the floor. She lifted the next bin off the shelf and was pleased to discover it was much lighter than the first. She pried off the top and found it was full of Ron's clothes.

Meredith lifted out the top item and held it up. It was one of Ron's favorite suit coats. A wave of memories rushed at her. He'd worn this coat so many Sundays at church, and at least once a week to work as well. The elbows were shiny from wear, and the cuffs were frayed. Meredith pulled the coat to her and felt the sting of tears spring up. It still smelled like him, like the sweet, spicy scent of his aftershave.

Meredith held the jacket close and let the tears stream down her cheeks. She felt silly, crying over a coat. But it wasn't really about the coat. *Ron*, she thought, *I miss you.* Her nose started to run, but luckily Ron always kept a pocket square in his jackets, so she pulled his handkerchief out and used it. He always like to be prepared for anything that might come up. He would have been so pleased to see his handkerchief come in handy now.

Meredith wasn't sure how long she sat there crying into his coat, but it finally occurred to her that she wasn't going to get any more sorting done that night. Reluctantly, she pushed herself up and folded the coat neatly and tucked it back into the bin.

She'd try again tomorrow, she decided. For now, she headed upstairs and started to get ready for bed.

But just as she was climbing under the covers, a thick book on her lap and GK curled up beside her, her cell phone rang. JULIA.

"Hello?"

"Are you asleep already?"

"Even if I had been, I wouldn't be anymore."

"Oh good. Listen up. I'm sitting outside a housing complex over on Wilmington Island—"

"Wait. What? You're where?"

"This is where Isabella came after work. I followed her out of her office building, into a grocery store, and then here. I'm waiting for her to come out, but she's been in there a long time, and there's nothing interesting happening. So I decided to do some research into our friend Earl Buford."

Meredith wasn't sure she would call him her friend, but she stayed quiet, waiting for Julia to continue.

"You'll never guess what I found out."

Chapter Four

Willie,

I am stuck in bed now on bed rest. Boo. There was some bleeding, and the doctor said I had something called placenta previa and that I have to stay in bed until the baby comes. I don't know how I am going to survive. But I am so glad Lou took me to the clinic. If I'd stuck with Daddy's plan of not seeing a doctor, the baby and I both could have died.

That lady I mentioned before, Lou, the one who took me to the clinic, says she's sure it's a boy, just like I think. She says you can tell because I'm carrying him high. Don't you want to meet your son, Willie? Please write back.

—R

Tuesday morning, Meredith studied the obituary Julia had found and then forwarded the night before, from the *Marietta Daily Journal*.

Eldan Vincent Buford, originally of Springfield, passed away January 6, 2017, after a long and valiant battle with cancer. Born November 1969, he served his country in the army for two decades and was a member of the local Rotary club. He is preceded in death by his wife, Marianne, and will be missed dearly. Services will be held at Maxwell's Funeral Home on January 10 at 4 p.m.

It had to be one of the Buford children, Meredith thought. The Buford house was outside of Springfield, but that was the closest town, and the name was probably used for simplicity. And Eldan was the right age—born two years after Earl and Daisy married, according to the wedding date listed in the Bible by the bedside. He would have been one of the older children in the photograph on the dresser. And he was mentioned in R's letter to Willie.

But he was gone, as was his wife, and no descendants were listed. Which meant that Meredith didn't have any leads. It was a good first step. They now knew the name of at least one of the children—probably two, in fact. But it didn't get them very far, unfortunately.

Meredith had sent Julia photos of the letters she'd taken from the house, and Julia promised to read them and look for any clues Meredith had missed. Hopefully Meredith would find something at the county offices that would help her make sense of it. After breakfast and her quiet time, she set off early. She figured she'd drive to Springfield, do some research in the Effingham County archives, and be back at her desk working on her insurance fraud case by noon.

The drive was quick, with most traffic headed the other way, into Savannah. She drove past the courthouse and found the red brick building that housed the county's property records, among other things. It was a grand building, with fluted columns and a decorated pediment and a rotunda on top, and it looked out of place surrounded by run-down single-story houses. Meredith found parking in the lot to one side of the building, and she made her way inside and studied the signs in the lobby, trying to work out where to start. She decided to head to the Effingham County Clerk's office, which was on the second floor. Meredith made her way up the grand staircase and found the office at the end of a carpeted hallway. She walked in and smiled at a woman about her age sitting at the front desk.

"Hello." The woman had short hair, and dangly earrings swung as she turned to welcome Meredith. "What can I help you with today?"

"Hi there. I'm hoping to learn what I can about a property over by Ebenezer Creek."

"Any chance you're asking about the old Buford place?" She smiled, waiting for an acknowledgment. Her voice had the deep, raspy sound of a longtime smoker.

"That's right. How did you know that?"

"Just a hunch." She smiled and held out her hand. "Theresa."

"Meredith." Meredith shook her hand.

"I heard that some city people were poking around there yesterday."

Meredith didn't even know how to respond. How had anyone known that they had been there? And how did Theresa find out? And what did she mean by "city people"?

"Now, I don't mean anything by it," she said, and Meredith saw that she wasn't trying to be unkind. "It's just that the neighbors notice when anyone goes by that old place."

Neighbors? She hadn't seen any houses anywhere around the old Buford place. "What neighbors?"

"Oh, there's lots of old places tucked away out there." Theresa waved her hand. "People who have been around for decades and don't have much excitement in their lives. They see a shiny SUV coming down the road, and it's the most exciting thing that's happened all year."

Meredith tried to wrap her head around this. Not only had people observed them out at the house yesterday, but word had traveled through the county.

"In any case, no one has been interested in that property for decades, and now that it's just been sold, here you are. If you wanted to buy it, you're too late, I'm afraid."

"Thankfully, I'm not interested in buying it," Meredith said. Especially now that she knew about the neighbors. "I've actually been hired by the woman who bought the property. She asked me to do some research into the place."

"What kind of research?" Theresa seemed genuinely interested to find out.

Meredith chose her words carefully. She couldn't come out and ask if the property was haunted. She imagined exactly how quickly that question would spread.

"I'm interested in finding out why it has stood empty for so long," she said.

"I don't know that there's any one answer," Theresa said. "Not too many people know what to do with a swampy piece of land out that way."

"I had heard something about rumors...." Meredith tried to phrase this carefully.

"Oh, you mean the ghosts?" Theresa laughed. "Yeah, that might have something to do with it too."

"So you've heard the rumors then?"

"Oh sure." Theresa nodded. "Don't mean I believe it, but sure, I've heard them."

"What do people say about it?" Meredith asked.

"Oh, you know, the usual. People see lights on in the house, when power was cut to the place ages ago. People have heard strange noises coming from the place, like it's moaning. That kind of thing."

"Do you think there's any truth to the rumors?"

Theresa just cocked her eyebrow and laughed again. Meredith decided to take a different approach.

"What happened to the owners? Why did the county take possession of the land in the first place?"

"The second question is easy. Taxes. Pretty much the only reason the county ever repossesses land around here." She shrugged. "The first, I can't tell you. That was before my time. I only moved to this area twenty years ago. All I know is that the county took possession of it in 1988, and no one has come asking about it in years."

Meredith thought this all through.

"If I wanted to find out more about the circumstances of the house being taken by the county, where would I find that?"

"You could fill out this records request," Theresa said, pulling a paper from a stack of photocopied sheets on her desk. She slid it across the counter. "Give us as much information as you know, and we'll see if we can find what you're looking for."

Meredith glanced down at the form. It looked like it had been photocopied so many times the letters were blurry. WE WILL TRY TO HAVE A RESPONSE TO YOU WITHIN 4–6 WEEKS, the form read.

"I'm sorry, but I was hoping to get the information a bit faster than this," Meredith said. "Are any of the records digitized?"

"'We're working on it,' is the line I'm supposed to give you. But the short answer is no. They were gonna hire someone to digitize everything, but the budget got cut, so…" She shrugged. Then, almost as an afterthought, she added, "The budget seems to shrink every year, and it's getting worse with fewer people working. All those drugs mean fewer people bringing in income to tax, and we get no money."

Meredith had read that the use of opioids and other painkillers was on the rise in this county, and she supposed that was what Theresa meant here. But she didn't want to believe the answer was no.

"The problem is, I was really hoping to find answers today," Meredith said. "Is there any way to get the records a bit sooner?"

"If you need it today, you could go to the Records Room and have a look around," Theresa said. "It's not the most organized, but maybe you'll get lucky."

"That would be wonderful," Meredith said.

Theresa directed her to a room in the basement, and Meredith found it at the end of a long hallway. She flipped on the light switch and saw that it was a stark room with a laminate table in the middle, as well as a couple of warped folding chairs. Around the edges of the room were dozens of metal filing cabinets. The fluorescent lights popped and hummed. Meredith set her purse down on the table and headed for the cabinet at the far end of the closest wall.

Property records was probably the place to start, she decided. Maybe she'd learn something about why the Bufords had lost the house. She scanned the handwritten labels until she found one that said PROPERTY TRANSFERS, 1960–2005. That seemed like a decent place to start, so she pulled out the drawer and studied the stuffed file folders. It took a minute to work out that it was arranged by date of transfer. Well, she knew the newspaper left on the dining room table had been from September 6, 1988. She guessed that the county had taken the house shortly after that. She flipped through the folders until she found the transfers for that year and then went through each one carefully until she found the right folder. She pulled it up triumphantly and carried it over to the table and took a seat before she opened it up.

She read through the forms and papers inside, wishing she had Julia's legal background to make sense of these contracts. But the result was clear enough: The property taxes on the house had not been paid, and after several years of trying to collect the growing debt, the house had been taken by the county. Taken for back taxes, just as Theresa had guessed. It seemed the county had held a tax sale, but there had been no bidders, so the county had retained ownership of the property.

Why had there been no bidders? It was a beautiful piece of land. Was it too expensive? Was that all there was to it? Were the rumored ghosts the reason no one had wanted to buy the Buford place? Or were people avoiding property because of something bad that had driven the family away? Or harmed them?

Scanning the rest of the documents in the folder, Meredith did learn something new: the property had been transferred to Earl in 1969, from Frank Leroy Buford, born 1920. So Earl had inherited the house.

Meredith returned the folder to the right drawer and located the files from 1969. After some digging, she found the property transfer documents and discovered that Earl had inherited the house and property from Frank—his father, Meredith guessed—after Frank passed away in January of 1969. But Frank had inherited the house from Ernest John Buford—*his* father?—in 1939.

Meredith dug around as far back as she could, but previous to 1935, the records were all lumped together in one drawer, with no real sense of order. Meredith looked through the drawers carefully, but she didn't find anything that had the name Buford on it. No matter, she thought. She'd learned that the Buford place had been a family homestead, passed from one generation to the next. Which made it all the more unlikely that Earl Buford would have let the house go willingly. What had happened to prevent him paying taxes on the place? Why had he been forced to give up the ancestral home?

Meredith decided the next step was finding out more about Earl and other members of the Buford family. Armed with Earl's birthdate—February 17, 1945, which she had learned from his driver's license—she located his birth certificate, and found that Frank Buford had indeed been Earl's father.

That was good information, but what she needed was to find out if Earl or Daisy Buford was still alive. If they were still out there, they could tell Meredith what had gone so terribly wrong.

She turned then to the section of the cabinets marked DEATH CERTIFICATES and scanned the date ranges listed. She had no idea if Earl had died, or when, and these were arranged by date. She looked through a few folders half-heartedly, and then she gave up. This would take forever.

She closed that drawer and looked around. If she could find Daisy and Earl's marriage certificates, that would give her Daisy's maiden name, and maybe she could find more of Daisy's family that way. She quickly discovered that the marriage certificate drawers were also arranged in chronological order, but that wasn't a problem this time. She'd seen their wedding date, inscribed in the front of Daisy's Bible. June 7, 1966. Meredith found the files for June 1966 and found a copy of Daisy and Earl's marriage certificate. Daisy Ruth Lowell had married Earl Walter Buford on June 7, 1966, at First Baptist Church in Springfield. Earl's address was given as 25 Ebenezer Road—the Buford place—while Daisy's home address was in Guyton, a small historic town to the west of Springfield. Daisy had been nineteen, and Earl twenty-one.

Meredith took a picture of the marriage certificate and then moved over to the birth records. She would try to track down the children and see if she could find any answers that way. She knew the name Eldan Vincent, from his obituary. But he was gone, so he would be no help. What were the names of the other five children, and were they still alive? Was one of them Willie, from the letters? She thought it was likely, but she couldn't be sure.

She knew that Eldan had been born in 1969, and she guessed he was one of the older children. She looked through the files, and there it was, in November of 1969—a birth certificate for Eldan Vincent Buford. The address listed was in Clyo, a town north of here. That must have been where Earl and Daisy were living before he inherited the house. Meredith felt a sense of triumph that faded as she realized that she didn't know what to do with this information. She needed the names of the other children. Was digging through all the records the best way to find them? And even if she found birth certificates for all the children, what good did that do her? She needed to know if they were still alive and how to contact them.

Meredith was growing frustrated. She knew a lot of people found work like this tedious, but she actually enjoyed digging through historical records. You could learn so much about a place and its people by going through forgotten primary documents like these. But today, she didn't seem to be getting anywhere, and she was starting to feel like she was wasting her time. Was there anything useful she could get from these documents?

She needed to get going soon. It was already almost noon, and she'd hoped to be back in Savannah by that point. She'd dig through a few more years' worth of files, she decided, and see if she could find any more of the children.

It didn't take long for her to find the birth certificate for William James Buford, born in January of 1967. His parents where Earl and Daisy Buford. Fifteen minutes later, she was about to give up when she came across a birth record for Nellie Elizabeth Buford, born December 23, 1970. Meredith considered the long rows of files.

Should she start digging through them, looking for marriage or property records?

She decided she'd try a shortcut, and she typed the name into the browser on her phone. The name William James Buford brought up a number of results, none of which were helpful. She typed in Nellie's name, and that pulled up—she couldn't believe it—a wedding announcement in the *Atlanta Journal Constitution* for Nellie Buford and David Allen Corporon.

A Google search for Nellie Corporon didn't turn up much of anything, but when she searched for David, she found his name featured on the website of a law firm based in Atlanta. He was probably in his fifties, she guessed, with graying brown hair and a mustache. She also found a social media profile for him and found him pictured several times with his arm around…oh. Well, that twentysomething blond couldn't be Nellie. Meredith assumed it was safe to say David and Nellie were no longer married.

But she now had a last name and a city. It couldn't be that hard to find contact information. The library often had out-of-town phone numbers. She would see if she could find a phone number for Nellie Corporon in an Atlanta phone book.

Meredith pushed herself up. She needed to get going. As fascinating as the empty Buford house was, she needed to focus on their other cases. She returned the files to the drawers and pushed them closed, and then she walked out of the room, trying to figure out her next step. It was past lunchtime now. She had a granola bar in her purse, but it shouldn't take her long to get back to Savannah at this time, and she could grab something there. Meredith turned onto Pine Street and started for the highway, but at the last minute, she didn't make the turn that would take her back to the main road. Instead, she turned to the east. She was all the way out here, after all. She was so close to the Buford place. She could just stop in and take a look at that cemetery quickly. It might be a way to find out more about the Bufords.

Before she even realized what she was doing, as if something else had pulled her, Meredith had entered the address into her GPS and was headed back to Ebenezer Creek.

Chapter Five

October 2, 1985

Willie,

By this point, I realize you're either not getting these letters or you don't care to respond. Still, this is your son, so I feel like I should keep you informed. The doctor says the baby is going to be big but that he's healthy. Lou says her son was really big when he was born and that it hurt a lot, but she says it was worth it for a strong healthy child. Lou has been looking out for me, making sure I go to my appointments. She's been so wonderful. You know I haven't been much for religion since Mama died, but I have been thanking God that Lou is in my life. I don't feel so alone with her. She's the only one who cares.

—R

Meredith pulled up in front of the Buford house and once again parked in the cleared space under the poplar trees. She'd wanted to take another look before she went to the cemetery, as if to reassure herself that the place was real, that she hadn't imagined the whole thing. She climbed out and caught the faint scent of smoke again. Was someone burning leaves? Whatever it was, it was faint. She looked up at the house. It must have been beautiful once, she thought, imagining a grand entryway flanked by stunning foliage. Now, all she saw were broken windows and rotting wood. *What happened here?* she thought. *What was it that drove these people away so suddenly?*

Meredith shook her head and turned, ready to head back to the car, when a flash in an upstairs window caught her eye. Was it…was there a light on up there? But as she tried to make sense of it, the light vanished.

What in the world…? Had she imagined it? There was no electricity in the house. Meredith was sure of that. And that flash had come from one of the children's rooms, which had definitely been empty yesterday. Had the sunlight hit the window in an odd way? But the house was nearly completely shaded, the yard overgrown as the forest took back the land. Suddenly, despite the warm day, Meredith felt chilled, and a shiver went through her. She should have just gone straight to the cemetery. She shouldn't have come here alone. As much as she loved old houses, this place was too creepy to face by herself.

Once again, she turned back to the car, but a sound through the trees off to the right caught her attention. The low hum of a motor drifted toward her from the direction of the creek. Meredith could see the silver surface of the creek through the trees, but there was no clear path down toward its edge. Brambles and vines covered the ground. Meredith looked down at her slacks and loafers, and then she took a deep breath and picked her way through the overgrown forest toward the water's edge. Moisture seeped into her shoes from the soggy, marshy soil, but the sound of the motor grew closer, and she hurried to catch the passing boat. Downstream, she saw the remains of what must have once been a dock, but she didn't trust what was left of the rotting wood to hold her weight. She thought about the reference to Willie's father going to the river. That dock had to be where he tied up his boat.

She swatted away bugs as she got as close to the swampy creek as she could before the earth gave way completely to water. The cypress and tupelo grew right out of the swamp, and she had to admit it was stunning. She saw a man in a silver metal dinghy coming up the creek toward her. Fishing rods were stacked at the front of the boat. Though his wide-brimmed hat shaded his face, she could see that he was watching her, his hand on the motor, waiting to see what she would do. Meredith raised her hand and called out, "Hello!"

The man nodded, and he let up on the motor and steered the boat toward her. When he was as close as he could get without running aground, he cut the motor.

"Hi there. I'm Meredith Bellefontaine," she said. Up close, she could see that he was probably in his sixties or seventies, and wiry, with tanned, leathery skin and a neatly trimmed silver beard. He wore a long-sleeved flannel shirt, even with the warm day—no doubt to protect himself from the insects that were starting to find her.

"Clem." He ducked his head just a bit, but he was still watching her.

"A friend of mine just bought the house here," she said, gesturing back toward the house. "The old Buford place. Do you know anything about the place?"

He didn't say anything for a moment, and the silence stretched out long enough that Meredith began to wonder if she should repeat the question. Then, finally, he spoke.

"The place has been empty for a long time." His drawl was thick but his words clear and his voice certain.

"I know," Meredith said. "And I've heard that some people around here believe it's haunted."

"Don't know about that," he said carefully. "I don't go in much for ghosts, personally. I suspect folks that think they see things out this way are not necessarily in the best state of mind anyway, if you get my drift."

"You mean they've been drinking," Meredith said.

"Among other things," the man said. "There's a lot of that around these parts these days. So, stories about strange noises and flashing lights… I just don't know as I'd put much stock in them, personally."

Meredith felt strangely relieved to hear him say it, though it didn't negate the fact that she'd thought she'd seen a strange light, and she hadn't been drinking or doing drugs.

"Have you lived around here long?" Meredith asked.

"All my life. Live just downstream a mile or so."

"Did you know the Buford family?"

"Can't say I did. Not personally, anyway. 'Course everyone around here knew *of* them, but we weren't what you'd call friendly."

The way he said it made her think there was plenty he wasn't saying. "What do you mean?"

"Oh, just that they weren't our kind of people." He paused again and was quiet long enough that she wasn't sure he was going to continue, but then he said, "They were a rough crowd."

"Oh? How so?"

"Just, in and out of trouble all the time. They were wild, you know? Didn't have much respect for rules and the way things are done here on the river. And there were so many kids running around, seemed like one of them was always up to something. Earl with his trips downriver to Savannah under the cover of night, as if he was fooling anyone. We didn't associate with them much."

"Earl went to Savannah at night?" Meredith asked. "Why?"

He didn't answer for a moment, and then he nodded. "Like I said. They were a rough crowd."

He wasn't going to elaborate, that was clear. She decided to try a different tactic.

"Do you know what happened to the Bufords?" She swatted a mosquito that had landed on her arm.

"I wouldn't know."

"Are any of them still around?"

"Not around here, least not that I know of."

"But there were all those kids. You don't know where any of them went?"

"I'm afraid I don't. I remember hearing that things went downhill after that mosquito sickness went through, but I don't know how much one had to do with the other."

"What mosquito sickness?"

He gave a small shrug. "There was some fancy medical name, but we all just called it the mosquito sickness. It made a lot of people sick around here in the mideighties. I heard the mom out there had it bad."

"Do you know what happened to her?" Could illness have been what took them all?

"I'm not sure. There were all kinds of rumors about the family, so it's hard to say what's true." He shrugged. "I wish I could tell you more, but, like I said, I don't really know. I just know that after a while, the whole place started to fall into ruin, and we didn't see the family around anymore. Don't know what happened. Honestly, plenty of folks around these parts weren't sad to see them go."

She let that sit for a moment, trying to make out whatever was behind his words. Was he saying people had been glad she'd died? They would have been glad if they'd all died?

"Well, I should get back," Clem said, tipping his hat.

Meredith thought quickly. This man had been around here his whole life. Even if he didn't know the Bufords, he might know other things. "Do you know of anyone named Mario?" she asked.

He thought a moment and shook his head. "Can't say I do." And then he turned on the boat motor and began to back away from the bank. Without another word, he steered the boat out into the creek and out of sight.

Meredith stood on the bank and watched him go, and then she turned and headed back toward the house. As she got closer, it emerged through the trees, a hulking white shell. Once she got to the driveway, she stood in front of it a moment and looked up at it. She didn't see any more flashes in the upstairs windows. Had that been just a trick of the sunlight? She couldn't say, but as she turned to go, she noticed that a window in another upstairs room stood wide open. She froze. Had it been open before? She tried to remember what the house had looked like when she'd seen it earlier, and she couldn't be sure. Wouldn't they have noticed if the window had been open when they were upstairs yesterday? She felt sure she would have, and she felt sure it hadn't been.

But if it hadn't been open before, why was it open now?

Meredith didn't think; she just turned and hopped into her car and backed out of the driveway. Once she had turned the car around and was headed back down the rutted road, she started to breathe easier. She had let her imagination get the best of her obviously. Surely that window had been open, and she just hadn't noticed it earlier. The glint in the window was just the sunlight filtering through the trees. The empty house was spooky, and she had let that overcome her rational nature. Her heartbeat slowed, and her breath returned to normal as she inched along the bumpy overgrown road, steering around the obvious holes and fallen branches.

As Meredith rounded the bend in the road, the little cemetery came into view, and she considered not turning off, given the suggestible state of her mind right now. But this was what she had come here for, after all, so she pulled the car over to the side of the road and parked it. There might have been a road here once, but it was long gone now. Meredith climbed through the brambles and weeds toward the walled-off clearing under the trees and slid over the waist-high fence. She really hadn't dressed for this day, she thought, as her feet landed on the other side. But once she looked around, she couldn't help the smile that spread across her face.

Meredith loved old cemeteries. She knew people who thought they were sad, depressing places, or even worse, creepy or boring, but Meredith had always appreciated the reminder that our time on earth was limited, and that we would all be returned to dust someday. It was a sobering reminder to live as best you could and serve the Lord faithfully while He gave you breath.

Aside from that reminder, few people realized what a gold mine of information an old cemetery could be, and the historian in her delighted in the sight of the tilting and moss-covered tombstones.

She surveyed the area, and it wasn't hard to deduce where the oldest graves were, in the far right corner of the cemetery. Meredith started there, slipping on plastic gloves before brushing aside dirt and moss.

SAMUEL CLARENCE BUFORD, 1837–1887.

That was it. There were none of the sentimental trappings that were so frequently found on historic tombstones. Why was that, she couldn't help wondering. What had he been like? Samuel was almost certainly the first generation of Bufords to live and die on this land. How had he come to this place, and what had he done while he was here? Had his family mourned him, and simply been expedient with the lettering? Or was there more to the story here? Meredith's mind was already swirling.

Next to Samuel's grave was a headstone that read IDA LAPIERE BUFORD, 1845–1892. BELOVED WIFE AND MOTHER. MAY GOD REST HER SOUL.

What had Ida's life been like? She had lived through the Civil War, probably here on this land.

Meredith moved on to the next set of tombstones, which appeared to be the sons of Ida and Samuel Buford, as well as of a

Frances Rawley Buford, who appeared to have been married to one of the sons. Had they only had sons? But then she quickly realized that any daughters would no doubt have been buried with their husbands' families, as Frances had been.

Meredith tried to trace the generations as they got close to the present day, but she quickly become confused, as so many members of the family had been gathered here. The saddest headstones were the children's graves. So many children hadn't made it past their third birthday. It was a difficult reminder of how delicate and dangerous life had been before modern medicine. She also noted how styles had changed through the years. Around the turn of the twentieth century, many of the headstones had been decorated with skulls, flowers, and long flowery verses. As the eras moved on, they were less elaborate and more to the point. Meredith took photos of each of the headstones in case they held any information she wasn't seeing now.

Meredith was in the newest row of headstones before she found names that were familiar. ERNEST JOHN BUFORD, 1892–1939. FRANK LEROY BUFORD, 1920–1969.

And then, DAISY LOWELL BUFORD. 1947–1986. TAKEN TOO SOON. MAY SHE REST IN PEACE.

She was gone, then. 1986. That was right around the time Clem had thought the mosquito-borne disease had hit and sickened the mother of the family. Had that been what had taken her? There was no way to know. But Meredith did know one thing. Earl was not here. Had he died and been buried somewhere else? Or was he still out there somewhere? Eldan was gone, but he wouldn't have been buried on this land, because the family didn't own it any longer.

But there was one more headstone, next to Daisy's.

LAUREL GRACE BUFORD, 1972–1980. SHE WILL NEVER BE
FORGOTTEN.

Laurel must have been Earl and Daisy's daughter. One of the
children in that photograph. Meredith's heart constricted to realize that she hadn't even made it to her ninth birthday. Meredith
wondered how she died, and how it must have affected her family to
lose her. It must have been devastating. Meredith knew that she would
never recover if something happened to one of her own children.
What a tragedy.

Daisy was the last Buford buried on this land, in 1986. They'd
lost the land and the home in 1988. What had happened to the rest
of the family?

Meredith pushed herself up, puzzling over the questions. She
now knew *when* Daisy had died but not *how*. Was whatever illness
had taken her what had driven the rest of the family away, seemingly
overnight? How was that possible? This wasn't the Civil War era.
They had modern hospitals in 1986, and penicillin. Was it possible
the disease had been so threatening it had chased the family away?

She didn't know. But she knew she needed to find out more about
whatever disease had swept through this area so many years ago.

Chapter Six

By the time Meredith got back to Savannah it was late afternoon and it almost didn't seem worthwhile to go into the office, but she decided to stop in and make sure there was nothing that needed her immediate attention. Then she would see if she could tail Aaron to Jimmy's again and figure out a way to get him to reveal himself.

"Long day, huh?" Carmen asked as Meredith stepped inside. "Did you find anything?"

"I'm not sure yet," Meredith said truthfully. "Maybe."

"Sounds about right," Carmen said. "You got two calls. One was from the school district, asking for a background check on a new substitute teacher." Carmen handed her the slip of paper she'd taken notes on. "And the other was from the insurance company checking to see if you had any updates on their fraud case."

"I haven't had much time to work on it," Meredith said, shaking her head. "I'll do some work on that case now and then head out to try to follow him."

"*Bueno.* And Julia was in earlier, but she's out now tailing the cheating wife. She also said she was going to go to the library to do some research on the Bufords if she had time."

"Let's hope she does," Meredith said. She took the notes from Carmen and made her way down the hall toward her office. After dropping her purse in one of the spare chairs, she checked her email, and then she opened the insurance fraud file folder. She tried to focus on the lines of numbers that ran down the page, but after a few minutes, her eyes were going blurry, and she realized her mind was elsewhere anyway. She was thinking about the Buford graveyard, trying to make sense of the names that filled that family cemetery. Finally, she set her file folder aside and took out a legal pad, turning to a clean sheet. She wrote the name *Earl Buford* in the middle and then wrote the name *Daisy Lowell Buford* next to him. Above him were Frank and Martha Buford. Were there other children of this generation? Meredith didn't know.

She did know—or at least, the family photo made her fairly sure—that Earl and Daisy had six children. She drew six lines from their names. She knew four of the children's names: Eldan, who had died three years ago; Willie, who was mentioned in letters; Nellie, whose name she'd found in the birth records, who had married David Corporon; and Laurel, who was buried in the family cemetery. She tried to come up with more names but couldn't. It was only a partially completed family tree, but it was the best she could do right now. She needed to find out more. How could she learn more about the Buford family?

Meredith closed her eyes and leaned back in her chair, and after a moment of silence, it came to her. How had she not thought of this before? Meredith scrolled through her phone and found Lacey's phone number.

Meredith had met Lacey Marven at many gatherings when Meredith had been the head of the Savannah Historical Society.

Lacey was involved with the Effingham County Historical Society, which wasn't as large or as formal as the Savannah Historical Society but still maintained a decent collection of materials about the region. Lacey was only in her midforties, but her family had been in the area for generations, as she would gladly tell you. She lived in an old plantation house that hadn't changed much in two hundred years, though now she and her family only kept a few chickens and her husband worked in finance. She had deep roots in the area, and if anyone would be able to find out about the Buford family, it would be her.

"Meredith?" Lacey said when she picked up the phone. Lacey had a thick drawl and a voice that dripped with honey.

"Hi, Lacey."

Lacey laughed and said, "How *are* you? How is everything going? How's the PI business?"

Meredith updated Lacey and told her about the latest event she'd attended with the Savannah Historical Society, a tea at the society's building to raise money for restoring the stained glass windows at a historic church in town. Then she got to the point of her call.

"I'm wondering if you might be able to help me find out about a family that used to live in the Ebenezer Creek area."

"Ooh, what a gorgeous area. But one with a dubious history. You know about the tragedy that happened there?"

"Yes, I do, and it was horrible," Meredith said.

"It took a long time for that historical marker to be erected," Lacey said. "But there was a tenacious group of volunteers who worked for it, and we finally got it done just in 2010."

"I heard that," Meredith said. "I'm glad it finally happened. It doesn't do us any good to ignore the parts of our history we'd rather hadn't happened. You can't learn from the past if you don't acknowledge what happened in the past."

"Isn't that the truth," Lacey said. "So tell me about this family in Ebenezer Creek."

"They were called the Bufords, and their house appears to have been abandoned. I'm trying to figure out what happened to the family."

"Do you have any names?"

"Earl and Daisy, plus their six kids. We know of a Willie, an Eldan, a Nellie, and a Laurel. But Laurel passed away as a child."

"What else do you know about them?"

Meredith shared what she'd learned at the county records room and what she'd picked up in the cemetery. "I'll email you the photos and copies of the records."

"I love it. Good old-fashioned research is my thing. I'll see if I can dig up anything about the family," Lacey promised. "We have old yearbooks, church directories, that kind of thing. I'm sure there's got to be some trace of them or someone who knows what happened. When do you need this by?"

"Oh, you know." Meredith laughed. "As soon as you can get it to me."

"Well, this sounds a whole heck of a lot more fun than the laundry I was about to start. I have a few hours before Mark gets home from work. I'll head over to the historical society now and see if I can find any reference to the family."

"Thank you so much. I appreciate it."

"Are you kidding me? I love this stuff."

Meredith might have felt bad, but she understood how thrilling it could be to dig through historic records searching for answers.

"I'll give you a call when I find something."

Meredith prayed she would.

October 23, 1985

Willie,

If you're getting this, then you already know Lou is looking for you. I can't leave this house, or I would do it myself, but since I can't, she says she will find you for me. I couldn't believe it when she told me she'd gone to your house and knocked on the door and demanded to know where you were. She told me that the guy who answered the door was big and unhelpful and made a rude comment about her skin color, but I wasn't sure if it was Eldan or your daddy until she told me he was young. Eldan, then. I wasn't surprised to hear that he didn't tell her anything, really. But she has promised to keep looking. I wonder if we'll find you first or if this letter will.

—R

Meredith went back to analyzing lines of insurance billing codes, and when she couldn't take it anymore she called Rachel and gave her an update. Then, just as Meredith was shutting down her computer and packing up to go tail Aaron, Julia came down the hallway.

"Oh good, you're still here," Julia said, slinging her purse off her shoulder. "I was hoping I could catch you."

Meredith smiled as Julia walked to her doorway. "Did you have a productive day?"

"Well, I got pictures of Isabella eating with three female friends after her tennis lesson. So, you know, not so much on that front." Julia came into the office and took a seat in one of the chairs. "But I did stop in at the library because I had a hunch."

"A hunch?"

"About those letters you took from the house."

"Did you figure out who R is?" Meredith wasn't sure how she would have, but it would be so helpful.

"No, but I did figure out who Lou is. The lady who helped her and took her to the doctor?"

Meredith nodded. "Who is it?"

"I remembered what you said about volunteers gathering signatures on petitions for decades, and I remembered that one of the letters had someone gathering signatures."

"Okay…" Where was she going with this?

"So I asked Maggie Lu if she knew the Bufords. I could tell the second I said the name I was right."

"Wait a minute. You're saying Magnolia Louvenia Clement King is the Lou from the letters?"

Maggie Lu was a retired teacher who now volunteered at the Carnegie Library. Julia and Meredith had met her a few months back and had gotten to know her better recently. She'd helped with several of their investigations.

"That's right. She didn't know much about the Bufords, but she had definite opinions."

Meredith tried to wrap her mind around this. "How in the world did you put that together?" Meredith had been staring at those letters for days and hadn't gotten there.

"Like I said, it was just a hunch. Remember that she used to go by Louvenia? I figured that since she had been a teacher, there was a chance she would have been one of the people trying to get that historical marker set up."

Meredith shook her head. "I would never have gotten there."

"That's why we make a good team." Julia smiled.

"So what did Maggie Lu say about the Bufords?"

"Hang on. Before I get to that, let me tell you what I discovered while I was searching through the archives of the *Effingham Herald*. It turns out the family was mentioned several times in the local press." Julia was reaching into her bag, and she pulled out a notebook.

"Really?" Perhaps Meredith shouldn't have been surprised by this, but somehow she was. From what she'd heard so far, they didn't seem like the kind of people who sat on civic councils and such.

"Well, don't get too excited. It's not great. Let's see." She flipped open her notebook. "The first mention I found of Earl Buford was in the police blotter section of the paper."

"Oh dear."

"Apparently Earl Buford was arrested for drunk and disorderly conduct on April 17, 1976."

"Is there any more information about the incident?"

"Only that he'd been threatening another man after a game of darts had escalated. This apparently took place outside an establishment called Tootsie's."

"Sounds like a classy joint."

"Judging by the number of times it shows up in the police blotter, I'd say it didn't attract the highest-caliber clientele."

"What else did you find?"

"Earl was also arrested for possession of illegal drugs a few years after that."

"Did it say what kind? How much? What happened to him?"

"It didn't say. I suppose we could look up court records, but I didn't get that far."

"Maybe we can do that down the line. For now, I think we're getting a fuller picture of what Earl was like."

"His son Jed was cut from the same cloth, apparently."

"Jed. That's one I hadn't gotten yet." Meredith wrote the name on a scrap of paper on her desk.

"Jedediah, technically. But apparently he went by Jed." Julia flipped to the next page in her notebook. "He was arrested in 1993 for grand theft. He broke into several garages and stole power tools."

"Yikes."

"This was before eBay, so he couldn't simply list them for sale online, though I imagine he found another way to unload them."

"Any other arrests?"

"None that made the papers. And the only other time I found a mention of any of the Bufords in the newspaper was when Daisy Buford took first place at the county fair for the entry in the flower-arranging category. Apparently she had quite a nice collection of poppies and chrysanthemums that wowed the judges."

"Huh. Didn't expect that."

"Yeah, well, people are complicated," Julia said. "They often do things you don't expect."

Meredith thought about this for a moment, and then she nodded. It was true. People had so many facets, and if you forgot that and focused only on negative sides of them, you could miss another aspect of a person's character. If nothing else, this job had taught her that.

"So what did you learn from Maggie Lu?"

"She didn't really tell me much," Julia said. "When I mentioned the Bufords in Ebenezer Creek, she got this funny look on her face."

"Like what?"

"Like she was disgusted but was trying not to show it. So I asked her if she knew them, and she crossed her arms over her chest and she nodded."

"Oh. She definitely does not like them."

"Right." Julia nodded. "That was clear."

Meredith tried to picture this. Maggie Lu was the kindest, gentlest woman she knew. She'd been through a lot, and there were so many things that could have turned her bitter or jaded, but Maggie Lu had a deep sense of peace and unshakeable faith about her. It was nearly impossible to imagine her harboring deep-seated dislike for anyone.

"So then I asked if she had helped a pregnant woman connected with the Bufords, and she said yes."

"Did she tell you who R was? Did they ever find Willie? Was the baby okay?"

"She didn't say. Not yet anyway. She said she wanted to show me something."

"What was it?"

Julia shrugged. "She was going to call when she found it."

"Huh." Meredith leaned back in her chair and thought about this. Maggie Lu was Lou. "Should we call her?"

"I don't know." Julia slipped her pen into the spiral binding and set her notebook on the desk. "I don't want to wait either. But I get the sense that if we rush her, it's not going to help our case. Let's give her a day or so and see if she gives us a call."

It was against everything in Meredith to simply sit back and wait, but she supposed Julia was probably right in this case.

"So how was your day?" Julia asked. "Did you learn anything about the Bufords?"

Meredith recounted what she'd learned at the records room, as well as what she'd found at the cemetery and her conversation with the neighbor on the creek.

"Wait. He said he thought they got sick?"

"He said some kind of mosquito sickness went through right in the mideighties. He didn't know any more about it, but it sounds like it could have been behind it, right? I mean, according to the headstone, Daisy passed in 1986, and he'd thought she had it bad."

"It does sound possible," Julia said. "Maybe Daisy got sick, and they got scared and all ran off and left."

"And left Daisy behind?" That didn't seem likely to Meredith.

"Probably not. Okay, well maybe after she died, they realized they were all in danger and ran off."

Meredith blew out a breath. "I mean, that seems a bit more likely, I suppose." She thought about it a moment. "But people don't die of mosquito-borne illness overnight, right? She would have been sick for a while. And what we saw in that house…" She shook her head. "Something scared them. Those people left without finishing breakfast. They just took everything and ran."

"More like took nothing and ran. They left behind all the things you would grab if you had only a few minutes to run for your life. You'd grab your wallet, your photos, your mother's Bible, precious letters…all the things they left behind."

"That's all true." Meredith nodded, acknowledging the truth of her words. "But still, they up and left, and quickly. And I can't help thinking the sickness that might have taken Daisy might have had something to do with it."

"We need to look into it." Julia twined a strand of silvery hair behind her ear. "What do you think it was? Malaria? West Nile? Zika?"

"I really don't know. I suppose we need to do some research to figure out what illness came through the area around that time. What do you think the best way to find out about that is? Maybe looking through obituaries? Or, I guess the newspaper would have reported on it. Maybe it means going back to the library and looking through the newspaper archives again."

She glanced at Julia and noticed she was packing her notebook into her purse again. "What are you doing right now?" Julia asked.

"Right now?" What was she talking about? "I'm sitting at my desk…?"

"I mean, after work. Do you have plans after work?"

"I was planning to tail my insurance fraud guy. Why?"

"That can wait. Let's go." Julia stood up and slung her purse over her shoulder.

"Go where?" Meredith didn't move. The insurance case could wait, but what was Julia dragging her along to?

"We're going to figure out what this mosquito illness was." She started out the door and then looked back and saw that Meredith was still sitting in her chair, trying to process. "Are you coming?"

Meredith didn't know what else to say. "I guess I'd better."

Chapter Seven

MEREDITH TAILED JULIA, AND SHE recognized where Julia was leading her when they were still several blocks away. She recognized the tree-lined streets and the charming, well-proportioned homes in one of the newer sections of town in the Moon River district.

"Why are we going to your house?" Meredith asked as soon as she recognized Julia's neighborhood.

"You want to know about an illness, right? Who better to ask than Beau?"

Julia's husband, Beau, was a retired anesthesiologist, so in some ways, he was exactly the right person to ask about a medical issue. But there was one problem.

"Julia. In 1986, Beau was in working in Atlanta, as were you, I might add. How would he know about a mosquito-borne virus in Effingham County?"

"Trust me. If Beau doesn't know, he'll know someone who does."

"All right." Meredith did trust Julia, and besides, she didn't have any better ideas. She followed Julia up the walkway. Meredith loved the historic character of her own home, but she was always charmed by Julia's two-story home. It was painted a soft moss green with black shutters, and it had the most decadent wraparound porch with ceiling fans and rocking chairs that just beckoned for sitting out and chatting on long summer evenings.

When they pulled into the driveway, she saw that the door to the detached garage was open, and Beau was crouched down inside the garage. Julia parked in the driveway and climbed out of the car. Meredith followed her, and Beau looked up as they approached.

"Hi there, Julia. Good evening, Meredith. Please forgive me for not greeting you properly."

Meredith loved Beau's proper Southern manners. She stepped forward now and saw that he was pulling small containers of live bait out of a cooler and transferring them to a small dorm-style refrigerator tucked into the garage. A tackle box and several fishing poles were laid out along the garage floor, and another cooler was open to reveal several silvery fish.

"That's quite all right." She didn't need worms on her hands. She nodded at the cooler of fish. "Looks like a good day on the water."

"Every day on the water is a good day on the water," Beau said, smiling. "But yes, we caught a lot today."

"How's Buddy doing?" Julia asked. Meredith recognized the name of one of Beau's fishing friends, a retired banker. On more than one occasion, Julia had shared dismayed stories of the shenanigans Buddy and Beau had gotten up to.

"He's good." Beau laughed. "His wife wants to get a dog, but he doesn't want the hassle. He told her, it's a dog or me."

"I can imagine how Linda responded."

"Yep. She said she chose the dog." Beau laughed again. "But he's not going."

Julia shook her head. Meredith pressed her lips together. She knew Linda and Buddy were joking, but a small part of her couldn't forget, no matter how much she tried to ignore it, that she would give just about anything for more time with Ron.

"We had a question for you," Julia said.

"Lucky for you, I'm full of answers."

"You're full of something," Julia said, shaking her head. "We want to know about a mosquito-borne illness that swept through the area around Ebenezer Creek, and maybe the greater Springfield area, in the mid-1980s."

"Well, now. That's an interesting question." He set the last of the containers into the refrigerator and pushed the door closed. "I'd have to do some research. Can you tell me anything else about it?"

"We think it was lethal, at least in one case," Meredith said.

"And there's a chance it was the kind of thing that came on quite quickly," Julia said. "Like, if someone got sick with it, it might make the others in the house run away before they caught it."

Beau nodded, taking it all in. "You're sure it comes from mosquitoes?"

"We're not sure about anything," Meredith said with a sigh. "But that's what I was told by someone who lives in the area."

"Well, it doesn't ring any bells, but I'll look at the medical journals and talk to a few people who lived in the area at the time to see if we can come up with any ideas about what it might have been."

"Thank you," Julia said. "We appreciate it." She glanced down at the fishing gear spread around. "Do you need any help?"

"No, I've got it covered," Beau said. "But maybe you could take those bass in before the heat gets to them. I was thinking we could have them fried tonight."

"Nice try. Not until your cholesterol goes down. Grilled it is."

Beau stuck out his bottom lip, and Julia laughed, and turned to Meredith. "Would you like to join us for dinner? We're having grilled bass."

"That sounds great, but I should head home." It was probably too late to tail Aaron now, but she could get back to Ron's boxes. Meredith knew the offer was sincere, but she didn't want to impose. Julia had had her over so often in the months after Ron's passing. "I have some things I need to take care of tonight."

***

Meredith headed up to Ron's workshop after eating a quick dinner of grilled pork chops and salad. She flipped on the overhead light, and the golf clubs came into view again. She needed to deal with those too. Ron had gotten the new set the Christmas before he passed, and they were quite a nice set. She supposed she should ask the boys if either of them wanted them, but Carter had just gotten new clubs for Christmas last year, and Chase didn't really play golf very much these days. If the boys didn't want them, maybe Beau would want them. Or perhaps her brother-in-law David. But then, she knew David already had a nice set, a new top-of-the-line collection Barb had spent too much time describing a few summers ago, and she knew that he didn't like clutter, so she doubted he'd want this used set. She didn't know if there was a market for used golf clubs, but she figured she could always list them on eBay. She should do the same thing with Ron's coin collection, probably. Meredith hauled the golf clubs downstairs and, in the warm lighting of her living room, took a few clubs out of the first bag and took photos of them, and then took pictures of the whole set. After she'd captured the set, she brought the coin collection downstairs and photographed that, and then she moved to the boxes of clothing again. She was resolved to make it through the first bin before giving up this time.

She lifted the top off the bin and pulled out the flannel shirt he'd loved to wear around the house.

Meredith squeezed her eyes shut and tried to hold back the tears that threatened to spill over. It was just a shirt. An old, out-of-shape one at that. But it still smelled like Ron.

Suddenly, a wave of exhaustion hit her, and she felt every one of her sixty-five years. It had been a long day, she reasoned. She should probably get to bed. She would feel better in the morning.

She'd gotten some good photographs. That was a start. It would do for today, and things would look brighter in the morning. She prayed they would, because she didn't know what else to do.

Chapter Eight

WEDNESDAY MORNING, MEREDITH WOKE UP before her alarm and climbed out of bed. She had slept well, and she was anxious to get moving. Carter was scheduled to arrive at nine, but she thought she might be able to get some work done before then. GK padded down the stairs after her, and she made her way to the kitchen and made a pot of coffee. After a quick breakfast of yogurt and granola and her devotional time, Meredith opened her laptop and pulled up a web page to a genealogy site she'd used to do research in the past. The advent of the online genealogy sites had been a huge boon to nerds like her who wanted to do research on families, and the more recent trend of using DNA to build out family trees had allowed her to locate more than one long-lost family member over the years.

Now, Meredith ran a search for the name Earl Buford. Based on what she knew of him, she thought it was unlikely he had used the site to build a family tree of his own, but she thought it was possible someone else in the family had built their own tree and included him. But a search for his name didn't turn up any results.

Next, she ran a search for the names Eldan Buford, William Buford, Nellie Buford, and Jedediah Buford. No dice. The name William Buford did turn up on one tree, but this William had been born in 1832 in Alabama, so Meredith knew this wasn't the same man.

DAISY LOWELL BUFORD, Meredith typed into the window next. The top result was for a woman named Daisy Lowell born in Georgia in 1947. Meredith clicked on the link. It was her.

Daisy Lowell was the daughter of Marshall and Catherine Calhoun Lowell, born in Springfield in 1947, Meredith learned. She was an only child and had grown up in Guyer, Georgia. Daisy's own marriage and children weren't recorded here, but she was linked to the Lowell family of Savannah, and the full family tree was recorded for the Lowells. Meredith couldn't help clicking a few links—the historian in her was just too tempted—and she was delighted to find that photos of several members had been posted, as well as other information like addresses and occupations. She had fun browsing the photos and imagining what life must have been like as a haberdasher or milliner in nineteenth-century Savannah.

But she needed to focus, so Meredith forced herself to stop browsing the links and narrow in on what she could learn from the site. She knew all about Daisy's ancestors, but how could that help her now? She stared at the screen, willing the symbols on the screen to rearrange themselves into a form that was useful, when she realized she should see who had built the tree in the first place. A link at the top of the page took her to a profile page for someone listed as AnnaMae Harrington. She was—Meredith did the mental gymnastics to figure the relationship out—a second cousin of the Buford kids. Her mother, Rose, had been Daisy's cousin. Meredith did not know how likely it was that she knew much, if anything, about Daisy or her family, but so far she was the closest living relative to any member of the Buford family she'd found, and she wasn't about to squander that. She found a link to contact AnnaMae, and Meredith sent her an email, asking for any information she had about the Buford family.

It was progress, but it still felt like a stretch, so Meredith decided to take a different tactic and try again. She pulled out her phone and found the photos she'd taken of the headstones in the cemetery, and then she ran searches on the names she'd found. CLEMENTINE TANGNEY BUFORD, she typed in. She was Earl's aunt, Meredith thought. But though her name showed up in a very extended Tangney family tree, it didn't link to the branch of the Buford family Meredith was looking for. IMOGENE HARPER BUFORD, she typed next, but had a similar result. A full tree for a Southern family, but it got her no closer to finding out what had happened to the Bufords. Orson William Buford, a brother of Earl's father, Frank. Thierny Walker Buford. Yates Parker Buford. Lyla Montgomery Buford. Meredith loved the old-fashioned Southern names, but she was getting through nearly all of the names she'd found in the cemetery and still hadn't found any link to the Bufords she was looking for.

Finally, though, with a search of the name Wesley Charles Buford, who, from what she could tell, was an uncle of Earl's, she found a tree that led her to a man named Bill Miller. Bill had built the family tree that included Wesley, who was his grandfather, and who was active on the site. Earl's wife and children weren't included on Bill's tree. Even though it was no doubt a stretch, Meredith composed an email to Bill, explaining that she was looking for information about one of his relatives, Earl Buford, and then sent it before she could change her mind.

She gulped the last bit of her coffee and glanced at the clock. Yikes. She'd need to get moving to be ready by the time Carter got here. She closed the lid of her laptop and got up to start her day.

***

Carter showed up at nine on the dot, just like Meredith knew he would. That boy was punctual, just like his dad had been. She'd called yesterday and asked him to show up a bit earlier so he could come out to the Buford place and help them move the couch this morning.

"Hi, honey," Meredith said, pulling him in for a hug. "How was the drive?"

"Hi, Mom." Carter's chestnut hair had a few gray strands in it, but he was looking trim and tan, no doubt the remnants of a recent vacation to Kiawah Island. He wore khakis and a polo shirt with running shoes—his version of banker-causal, she supposed. "The drive was fine. I hit a bit of traffic, but that's to be expected at this time of day." Carter stepped inside and closed the door behind him. "How are you doing?"

"I'm fine. Busy, but good." Meredith gestured to the kitchen. "Can I get you a cup of coffee?"

"Nah, I had some on the way." He slid his keys into the pocket of his pants. "Besides, if we're headed out to the boonies, we'd better get going so we can make it back in time for my lunch."

"All right," Meredith said. "Let's get the bookcase loaded into your car, and then Julia will come pick us up and take us out that way."

"Great. It's in the spare room?"

"That's right," Meredith said. She showed Carter where the bookcase was.

"I've always loved this bookcase," Carter said, gazing at the four glass-fronted cabinets.

"Well, I know your dad wanted you to have it," Meredith said. "And it's not doing anyone any good in here."

Carter looked around the room. "It looks like you've been going through Dad's things." There was a look on his face that she couldn't read.

"I decided it's time. It's silly to have all this stuff just sitting around here." But her voice cracked on the last syllable, and Meredith pressed her lips together firmly.

Carter watched her for a moment and then said, "It's okay if you're not ready, Mom."

He said it gently, tenderly, but still the words made Meredith feel unexpectedly defensive.

"It's okay," she said. "This is something that needs to be done."

"Yes," Carter said, "but that doesn't necessarily mean it has to be done now."

Meredith didn't know how to answer that. It had been two years. If she wasn't ready now, she might never be.

"Losing Dad was a big deal," Carter said. "For all of us." And then, a moment later, "It's okay if you need some more time, is all I'm saying. There's no rush." For a moment, he looked like he was going to say more, but then he shook his head. "I mean, except for this bookcase, of course. I'm taking this bookcase now."

He grinned, and it somehow lightened the air, which had become heavy and thick over the past few minutes.

"Let me help you," Meredith said, but before she could reach for it, he somehow leveraged it against his body weight and carried it down the steps on his own.

"Wow. It looks like all those push-ups are paying off," she said once he'd laid it flat in the back of his SUV.

"It's about time." He pushed the back liftgate of the SUV down. "All right then. Do we need to call Julia?"

"She's already on her way," Meredith said. "She should be here in just a—"

She stopped as Julia's car rounded the corner and pulled up in back of Meredith's house.

"Well then," Carter said. "That's good service."

"Hi, Carter!" Julia rolled down the window and shouted out to them.

"Hi there, Aunt Julia."

"You guys ready to go?" Julia asked.

"One minute. Let me run in and get my purse," Meredith said. She was back in a moment and climbed into the passenger seat. Carter was already in the back of the car, chatting with Julia about his vacation.

"It was hard to get Kinsley off the beach," Carter was saying. "But Kaden got really into tennis, and we had a great time knocking the balls around on the courts. And the food was spectacular."

"It sounds like an awesome vacation," Julia said.

"You should see the beach there. It's so beautiful," Meredith said, though she'd only seen the pictures.

Julia put the car in gear and pulled away from the curb. "How would you feel about a haunted hotel, Carter? Would you stay someplace where there were rumored to be ghosts?"

"What?" Carter laughed. "I mean, maybe. How haunted are we talking? Like, *The Shining* haunted? Or just, like, a few spooky things that happen every now and again? A friendly ghost?"

"I suppose I hadn't realized there were levels," Julia said as she pulled out into traffic. "Maybe somewhere in between?"

Carter shrugged. "I don't know that I'd be able to convince Sherri Lynn to come with me, but I might be intrigued, personally."

"We're supposed to be convincing Rachel that the place is *not* haunted," Meredith said.

Julia shrugged. "I don't think it is, but I'm testing out the idea to see if she should embrace the rumors after all. As a marketing strategy."

"The only problem is"—Meredith glanced back at her son— "ghosts aren't real."

"I know that," Carter said. "But it's interesting anyway."

"It's definitely interesting," Meredith said, and then, by way of warning him what he was about to see, she explained how it seemed as if the family had just vanished.

"Wait. Like alien abduction kind of disappearance?" Carter had his head tilted.

"Well, there's one theory we hadn't considered." Julia laughed. "Add 'aliens' to our list, Mere."

"I don't think so." She grimaced. "We were thinking maybe there was some kind of threat to the family that made them drop everything and run. Or maybe it was something more like a sickness. We think the mother died of a mosquito illness, and we wondered if maybe it drove the others off as well."

"Speaking of which, Beau did some research for us." Julia braked for a red light, but it turned green before she stopped fully. "He has a theory."

"About the disease?" Meredith asked.

"Exactly." Julia crossed the intersection and continued down the road, which was bordered by shopping centers and gas stations as they left the city. "He talked to some friends and checked in his big fat medical journals—which, it turns out, are good for more than just curing insomnia, like I always thought—and he says there was an outbreak of Eastern equine encephalitis in that area in the summer of 1986."

"An outbreak of what?" Carter asked from the back seat.

"Eastern equine encephalitis. I know, it sounds like a disease for horses, but it's not. I guess it started with horses or something, but apparently it's spread by mosquitoes and causes high fever, paralysis, and even death."

"That sounds awful."

"It's pretty bad. Beau says it's often treatable with medication, but if someone doesn't get proper treatment in a timely manner, it can be deadly."

"Daisy died in 1986," Meredith said.

"Right. So it's possible—dare I say likely?—that this is what took her. That would line up with what you heard from the neighbor on the river."

"Judging by what we know of the family, it seems likely they didn't have great medical care," Meredith said.

"And she had six kids, right?" Carter asked. Meredith and Julia both nodded. "If Sherri Lynn is any indication, a mother is the last one in the family to go to the doctor. So if she was sick, there's a good chance she wouldn't go for treatment until it was too late."

"Right," Julia said. "So, without access to medical records or any other actual evidence, let's assume that Eastern equine encephalitis is what killed her. Where does that get us?"

"Nowhere, really." Meredith sighed. "Because the newspaper in the house was from 1988, so we know they weren't running from the sickness that killed her two years earlier."

"Which basically rules out the theory that disease chased them away."

"I suppose we shouldn't cross it off the list entirely," Julia said. "Maybe there was some other illness. But it does seem pretty unlikely." She signaled and changed lanes. "You said you looked into the possibility that they were all killed?"

"Oh my goodness." Cater laughed uncomfortably. "This has gotten dark. I don't know how I feel about you being mixed up in something like this, Mom."

Meredith waved off his concern. "It would have been decades ago, if it were true, but I don't think it is. I didn't find anything online about a family being murdered."

"And there was no mention in the newspapers when I searched for the Bufords," Julia said. "It seems like that's the kind of thing that would have come up in the papers."

"So let's assume that wasn't what happened," Meredith said.

"Thank goodness," Julia added.

"I really think we're looking at blackmail or extortion of some kind," Meredith said. "Like we thought when we found that note in Earl's wallet."

"I suppose that's the most likely possibility," Julia said. "So we need to find out who Mario is."

"And why Earl Buford owed him money," Meredith added.

"It might have something to do with Willie's baby. Maybe her family threatened them. Or the law got behind her, or something."

"And they all ran off so one of the kids didn't have to pay child support?" Julia asked.

"I don't know. Maybe." But it sure sounded implausible when she said it like that. "I'm just trying to think of ideas here."

"Have you considered the possibility of zombies?" Carter asked. "Zombie attack would explain how the whole family disappeared so quickly."

Both women froze. Meredith turned back toward him and saw that he was smiling. He was joking.

"Now that's an interesting idea," Meredith said. "One we hadn't considered."

"There are a number of informative zombie movies out there that could provide context. I'd be happy to make a list for research purposes."

Julia was shaking her head. "You're officially in charge of that line of inquiry," she said.

"Hey. It's not too far off mass murder, which you actually were considering," Carter said, shrugging. "Or ghosts. What's the difference between checking for ghosts and checking for zombies?"

"You know, the boy's got a point."

"Who invited you along?" Meredith said, laughing. "Now, can we please stop talking about these things? If we're going to go into that house, I can't think about ghosts or zombies or anything of the sort."

Julia changed the subject and gave Meredith an update on Isabella. Julia had followed her to a craft store the day before.

"What would she be doing there?" Meredith asked. "She doesn't seem like the crafty type, does she?"

"I suppose it depends on what you mean by crafty," Julia said with a smirk. "All I know is that she was in there for about half an hour and came out with bulging bags."

"What did she buy?" Meredith tried to think about what that could be. "Fabric? Batting?"

"My guess was yarn, but I can't say for sure."

"Maybe she's taking up knitting."

They bantered about what Isabella might be up to, but as Julia pulled off the larger road and onto the dirt and gravel road that threaded through the trees, the car fell silent.

"Wow," Carter said when he caught his first glimpse of the creek through the trees. "That's incredible."

The sight of the massive tupelo and sweetgum trees rising straight out of the swamp truly was so unexpected it was stunning. Meredith guessed that no matter how many times she saw it, she would never get tired of it.

"The family cemetery is coming up just over there," Meredith said, pointing to the stone wall around the headstones. "It's fascinating."

"Leave it to you to find a graveyard fun," Carter said.

"There's so much you can learn about the past and the people who lived through it if you just pay attention," Meredith said.

"I know, I know. And what happens in a place is a part of it forever, and if you forget history you're doomed to repeat it, and all that." He smiled at her. "I remember."

As they rounded the last bend and the house came into sight, Carter let out a low whistle. "Okay, I'm resurrecting my theory about zombies. This definitely looks like the kind of place a zombie attack would have happened."

"It's even better inside," Meredith said, hopping out of the car. The sound of the car doors closing echoed in the still air. "Come see."

They led Carter inside, and he seemed as surprised and confused by the state of the old mansion as they had been.

"It looks like they just...left." He gestured at the molded-over mug and carton of orange juice. "They didn't put away their breakfast dishes."

Carter was not exactly the neatest man in the world and had left his dishes out more times than she could count growing up, which is how Meredith knew he was seeing the strangeness of this house.

"Exactly," Meredith said. "Which is why we're so confused about what happened to them."

Carter nodded, his eyes moving from the peeling wallpaper to the rotting curtains to the warped floorboards.

"Wow," was all he said.

Meredith and Julia led him through the kitchen to the upended couch, which was still pushed up against the basement door.

"Maybe it's best to leave it where it is," Carter said. "You don't know what's down there."

"That's exactly why we want to get in there," Julia said. "To see what's down there."

"It might not be safe. I don't want you in danger, Mom."

"That's very kind," Meredith said. "But it's going to be fine. And Julia's going to get into that basement one way or another. I'd prefer if you helped, because I don't know what method she's going to resort to to get this door open otherwise."

"All right." Carter sighed.

"Somebody made this couch to last," Carter said, tugging the base of the couch toward himself. His cheeks were turning pink. Meredith and Julia positioned themselves on the far end and leaned their body weight against it while Carter pulled. It slid a half inch, at most.

"Let's try it again," Carter said. They all worked together, and finally, just when Meredith was about to give up, the thing slid out of the way.

"Someone really didn't want anyone to go down to the basement," Julia said.

"Right." Small beads of sweat had popped up on Carter's upper lip and forehead. "Which is why I don't think you should."

"You couldn't stop me now," Meredith said. Now that they were this close, she found herself ridiculously curious. What was hidden down there? She had to know now.

"Why don't I go down first and check it out?" Carter asked.

"Not on your life," Julia said. She put her hand on the doorknob, and Meredith held her breath while she turned the handle. "It's locked."

"Hang on." Meredith moved forward and crouched down to take a look. It was an old-fashioned decorated metal knob—brass, most likely—with a carved faceplate around the keyhole. "You haven't seen a key around here anywhere, have you?"

"A key?" Carter's eyebrows drew together.

"A skeleton key, it looks like. One of those old-fashioned ones with the two teeth at the end."

"I've seen a lot of things around here, but I didn't see a key." Julia blew out a breath. "We can't be this close and not get in. Can we break the door down?"

"Hang on. I don't think we need to do that." Meredith had taken a class when she was getting her PI license that had covered situations like this. "Julia, could you go upstairs and get a wire coat hanger from one of the bedrooms?"

"Okay." Julia nodded, but then she hesitated. "But I'm not going up there alone."

"I'll come with you." Carter led her up the stairs, and while they were gone, Meredith used the flashlight app on her phone to peer into the keyhole. It looked pretty standard, from what she could tell. When Carter and Julia returned, Meredith took the coat hanger and straightened it out, and then she bent the end down so it was roughly the same shape as a key. She carefully fitted it into the keyhole. It took a few tries, but she eventually felt resistance on the wire. That meant it was in place. Then, she turned the wire. The lock was stiff, but it turned. She heard a click as the lock bolt moved into the open position.

"Mom. Where did you learn to do that?" Carter was laughing and shaking his head.

"Don't you underestimate your old mom," Julia said. "She's a professional."

"Who are you calling old?" Meredith didn't know whether to laugh or be offended. She stood and moved out of the way.

"Let's do this," Julia said. She put her hand on the door handle, and this time, it turned. She pulled on the door, and it creaked open.

"I'll go down first," Carter said. "To make sure the steps are stable."

Meredith wanted to argue, to say that she and Julia were not some wilting Southern belles and could take care of themselves, thank you very much, but truthfully, she was grateful for her son for volunteering.

Meredith turned the flashlight app on her phone back on, and Carter pulled out his own phone and did the same. As he stepped down, she moved toward the top stair, bracing herself for a wave of putrid air. But it wasn't as bad as she had thought. The air was stagnant and stale, smelling of mold and must and smoke and some kind of rot. But it wasn't the unbearable stench of decaying bodies or—

Meredith stopped herself there. What had she gotten herself into that she'd honestly been expecting to find corpses in the basement?

"There's a bannister here," she called back to Julia, stepping down onto the first wooden stair.

"Are the steps stable?" Julia asked.

"They're fine," Carter said. "They'll hold."

Meredith wasn't sure she was ready to see whatever was down here, but slowly, as she went down step-by-step, the basement came into view.

Chapter Nine

November 1, 1985

Willie,

Lou told me that you are one difficult man to track down. She is asking people where you are. She has promised me that she will find you, and I hope she's right. Where are you, Willie?

—R

"What is it? What do you see?" Julia called from behind.

"I'm not sure," Meredith admitted. It was cooler down here, and as she descended, Meredith saw the stone foundation of the home appear, as well as a vintage washer and dryer and dozens of cardboard boxes. She saw rusted bikes and garden tools. Everything was covered in thick layers of cobwebs, and there was a distinct smell that suggested at least one small animal had died down here. She got to the dirt floor and shined her flashlight around, looking for...she didn't know what, exactly. Julia stepped down beside her and looked around, shaking her head.

"It just looks like a basement," Julia said, echoing the thought that was going through Meredith's head.

They could see tiny shafts of light coming in through the cellar doors, which she knew were nailed shut on the outside.

"We're missing something. There has to be a reason it was blocked off," Meredith said. She shined her light around and saw a hulking coal stove. Black coal dust littered the ground around it, though she guessed coal hadn't been used to heat this home in generations.

Carter had wandered toward the far side of the open space, shining his flashlight over a rusted metal boat hull. He lifted up the edge, and insects scurried away, but all that was underneath was a stack of paddles.

Meredith moved over to take a look at the cardboard boxes, but they seemed to contain nothing more frightening than old clothes. She shined her flashlight over them, trying to make out what was what, when something caught her attention. Upstairs. It almost sounded like… But it couldn't be footsteps. She listened again, but the noise, whatever it had been, was gone.

"I don't see anything over here," Julia called from the corner with the appliances. "Just old machines."

Meredith shook her head. "Is it possible that there's nothing here?" It didn't make sense, though. "But why would the basement be blocked off?"

"There's something over here," Carter said. He kicked at an object on the ground. Both Julia and Meredith hurried over to the corner where he stood, looking down. Meredith shined her light on the ground and saw some sort of small pipe.

"Tobacco?" Julia asked. Tobacco had been a big money crop in these parts many years ago, mainly cultivated with the unpaid labor of generations of enslaved people.

"No. It's not that kind of pipe," Carter said. He kicked a spoon lying next to it gently with his toe.

That meant it was for drugs. Meredith had seen enough movies to know that. "How did you know that?" She laughed.

Carter held up his hands. "Don't worry, Mom. Not from personal experience. I'm not into crack, I promise. I've just seen a lot of television shows."

"Earl was arrested for multiple drug offenses," Julia said. "We know that. So I guess it's not all that surprising to find drug paraphernalia here."

"Assuming it was Earl, or someone else in the family, who left this here," Carter said. "Who knows when that couch was shoved in front of the door? It could have been someone down here years later smoking who thought they saw something strange and blocked it off."

Julia nodded. "True."

"We don't know if this is Earl's—crack pipe?" Meredith looked at Carter, who nodded. "We don't know if this is Earl's crack pipe or not, but we know he was arrested on drug charges more than once. I think we need to be looking into whether drugs had anything to do with the family's disappearance."

"You mean, maybe the money Earl was supposed to turn over at Mario's had to do with drugs?" Julia asked.

"Maybe." Meredith tried to think through possible scenarios. "Or maybe he was distributing some kind of drugs and got in over his head. Maybe he got involved with the wrong kind of people and double-crossed them or owed them money or…I don't know. It could have been all kinds of things, honestly." She thought about television shows she'd seen, where drug deals gone wrong had led to all kinds of violent and gruesome deaths. "But whatever the issue was, I think it's possible someone threatened the family, someone who meant it, and the family had to disappear."

"Maybe they were laundering money and got found out," Carter said. "Or mismanaged the money they were supposed to pass up the chain and got caught short."

"It's certainly possible," Julia said. She had started to walk toward the corner of the room, her flashlight trained on the ground. "That's the kind of threat—a warning from a powerful drug lord or a foreign cartel—that would lead a family to up and go suddenly."

Part of Meredith couldn't believe they were having this conversation. Maybe they all watched too much television.

"Hey, wait."

Meredith turned and saw that Julia was looking at something on the ground in the far corner of the basement.

"Check this out."

Both Carter and Meredith hurried over, and they saw that she had shined her light onto the remains of what looked like a small fire, as well as a sleeping bag and two blankets. Two empty cans of beans were nearby, and there was soot on the ceiling.

"None of this stuff is dusty," Carter said. "This was left here recently."

"Someone has been camping out in the basement?" Meredith tried to make sense of this. "But the basement was blocked off. How could someone have gotten in?"

"I have no idea—" Julia started, but then she froze.

There it was again. The unmistakable sound of footsteps, walking over the floorboards above them.

"Do you guys hear that?" Julia asked.

Meredith could tell by Carter's face that he had heard it too.

"Is that footsteps?" Carter asked.

Lord, help us. In the split second before she ran for the stairs, a dozen scenarios raced through Meredith's head. But the worst one, the one that motivated her sprint for the stairs, was the idea that someone was walking around upstairs and was about to lock them in the basement.

No one told the others to run, but neither of them hesitated. Julia got to the stairs first, and she and Carter clambered up, with Meredith just a few steps behind them. Julia made it to the first floor, and by the time Meredith spilled out behind them, both Carter and Julia were looking around, eyes wide.

"Come out!" Carter was calling in his deepest voice. "We know you're here!"

"Who is it?" Julia called out.

Meredith was already looking around for something she could use as a weapon.

"Why don't you two wait outside?" Carter suggested quietly.

"Uh-uh." Julia shook her head. "No way. We're in this together."

Meredith was glad Julia had said it, because she didn't know if she would have had the courage to say those words herself. But they did stay behind Carter as he walked into the kitchen. There was no sign of anyone. Meredith tried to keep her breathing as normal as possible, but her heart pounded and she was sweating. Carter went from the kitchen to the dining room, Julia and Meredith following closely behind, and then into the hallway and parlor. They checked closets and behind every open door, but there was no one.

"We closed the front door behind us when we came in," Meredith said, pointing at the door that was still shut tight. "I didn't hear it open."

"We might not have heard it in the basement," Julia said.

"It doesn't seem like anyone went out that way," Carter said. "And the back is not an option."

"Upstairs," Julia whispered, and reluctantly, Meredith followed her and Carter. If someone was hiding out upstairs, he would be trapped when the three of them went up. But the three of them could also be trapped up those stairs, Meredith thought. Still, Carter was already heading up, with Julia close behind him. They searched through every room, and there was no sign of anyone.

"We're not crazy, right?" Julia asked when they had gathered back in the kitchen. "I definitely heard footsteps."

"I could have sworn I did too," Carter said. "But I don't see how it's possible."

"I heard them before," Meredith said quietly. "While we were downstairs."

"I did too," Julia said. "But I thought it was just my mind playing tricks on me."

"All of our minds were playing tricks on us, if that's the case," Carter said. "Because we didn't all imagine that."

"Could someone have been here and escaped without us seeing them?" Julia's rational mind was trying to make sense of what seemed like an impossible situation. "Wouldn't we have heard someone running toward the door?"

"Maybe not, in our haste to get up the stairs," Carter said. "They would have had to sprint off into the woods pretty quickly, but maybe they did."

"We know someone was using the basement somehow," Julia said.

Meredith got shivers, thinking that someone else had been there in the house with them. Who was it? Had they been here before the three of them had arrived? Or had he come in while they were here? They couldn't have missed the car parked in the driveway. They had to know someone was here. Why had they come in, and what did they want?

"That has to be it," Julia said. "I mean, what's the alternative?"

Meredith couldn't bring herself to consider the alternative.

Carter cleared his throat. "If you're suggesting it might have been a ghost... Well, I hate to be the voice of reason here, but ghosts don't exist."

Meredith looked over at Julia and met her eye. They both agreed. But in that case, what was going on?

Chapter Ten

Meredith couldn't believe she and Julia were headed back to Ebenezer Creek for the fourth day in a row. After the unexplained footsteps in the Buford house the day before, they'd had to drive back to Savannah so Carter could make his lunch meeting. And, if she was honest, she hadn't wanted to stick around. Today, after a good night's sleep and a cup of coffee, she knew there had to be a rational explanation for the sounds they'd heard, but yesterday, she had wanted nothing more than to get away from that house.

She'd spent Wednesday afternoon tailing Aaron Whitaker, hoping to catch him doing anything that would show that he wasn't really hurt, but he'd spent most of the afternoon parked on a stool in Jimmy's. Again, Meredith didn't follow him inside, but a phone call to the bartender after he left offered up the insight that he had stayed on his familiar stool downing pint after pint of cheap beer, which Meredith knew he could do injured or not. She'd have to keep after him.

She'd also called Chase, who lived in Atlanta, and asked him to look up a phone number for Nellie Corporon in his local phone book. He claimed not to own a phone book but did an online search for her and found a number that went to voice mail for a Nellie Corporon. So far Meredith hadn't gotten a call back, but she'd keep trying.

And she'd talked with Quin, who had invited her out to dinner tonight. Meredith was already looking forward to seeing him.

While she was waiting outside the bar, she'd also come up with a plan, and this morning, she and Julia had set out for Ebenezer Creek with a clear mission in mind.

"So what do you know about these neighbors?" Julia asked. She was in the passenger seat this time, while Meredith navigated to the first home. She'd used Google Earth to locate every home within a mile of the Buford place, and she'd mapped out a route to visit each of them today. Theresa at the county office had told her that the neighbors had known when the city folks had shown up at the house; if they knew that much, someone out there had to know what happened to the Bufords.

"Almost nothing," Meredith admitted. "I was able to get addresses from Google Earth. If I'd been at the records room I could have found out more, but I was limited to what I could find online while I sat outside Jimmy's." She shrugged. "I was able to find the names of a few of the property owners by googling the addresses, but even that didn't give me a lot to go on, since a lot of these people are not well represented on the internet."

"Not surprising really," Julia said. "If you're living this far out, you're probably okay with being off the grid."

"Whether or not it's your choice, you sort of are, by default," Meredith said, nodding. "But we'll see what we can find."

Julia talked about how the day before she'd seen Isabella meet up with a man who turned out to be her brother, and it wasn't long before they pulled into the driveway of a log cabin-style home with window boxes filled with bright pink pansies and an American flag swinging in the breeze. A neatly mown lawn surrounded the house, sloping up to the tree line at the back. As the crow flies, it was only a half mile or so from the Buford place, but it was accessible only from a road that didn't connect to Ebenezer Road, and it felt a whole world apart.

"Wow. This is a little different," Julia said as she stepped out of the car. A little white dog bounced up and down in the front window.

"Shall we?" Meredith led her up the crushed gravel path, bordered by pots of geraniums, and up the steps to the front door. Julia rang the doorbell, and a few minutes later, the door was opened by a woman with white hair. She looked up at them through thick glasses. Meredith guessed her to be in her seventies, though it was hard to say.

"Hello?" She looked from Meredith to Julia and back again. "If you're selling Avon, you're a few decades too late. No miracle cream is going to make me look young again."

Meredith didn't know how to respond, but then the woman laughed, and Julia laughed as well, so Meredith let out her breath.

"No Avon today, unfortunately," Julia said with a smile. "We wondered if we could ask you a few questions. Have you lived around this area long?"

"Only about forty years," she said with a grin. "Does that count?"

"I would say that counts as a long time," Meredith said. "In that case, did you know the Buford family?"

The woman's eyes narrowed, and she nodded slowly. "A bit. They're the closest neighbors, so we interacted with them some. Though not very often, if I could help it."

"I take it you didn't necessarily get along with them?" Julia asked.

"Can I ask what this is all about?" The woman, who had seemed so open and jokey before, was more guarded since they'd mentioned the Bufords, Meredith noted.

"We're working with a young woman who recently bought the property," Julia said, leaving out the possibility of a hotel in the area. They'd decided not to talk about that, since there was no telling what the neighbors would say. "And we're trying to help her figure out more about the history of the property and the family who lived there."

"You mean you're trying to find out if the house is haunted?" She cocked an eyebrow.

"We're trying to figure out why those rumors started," Meredith admitted. "But we're also interested in learning more about the family."

The woman looked back and forth between them again and then nodded. "You might as well come in." She pulled back the door to let them step in. "I'm Edna Fink."

"Meredith Bellefontaine. And this is my friend Julia Foley."

They stepped into the living room, which had cream-colored carpeting and tufted blue upholstered furniture topped with lace doilies. The walls were hung with paintings of landscapes and sunsets. Edna gestured for them to sit on the couch, while she sat in an armchair. A television was showing a home shopping channel on silent, and a woman with manicured fingernails displayed a gold necklace.

"Those are beautiful pictures." Julia gestured to the paintings behind Edna.

"Thank you." Edna sat up straighter. "I did them myself. Decided I needed a hobby once George passed."

"You did those?" Julia asked. "Wow. You're quite talented."

Meredith couldn't tell if Julia really loved the pictures or if she was just laying it on thick to win Edna over, but Edna seemed pleased.

"Thank you," she said, resettling herself in the chair. "Now, you wanted to know whether the Buford place is haunted," Edna said. "The answer is no. Kids go out there and poke around and use flashlights because there's no power out there, and when folks see it from the river, they assume the worst."

"But the doors are nailed shut," Julia said.

Or they had been, until she'd pried them open. And the thick dust inside showed no one had been in there in years.

There hadn't been anyone inside the house when Meredith had seen that flash of light in the upstairs window—had there? She supposed that the front door had been unbolted by that point, and she hadn't gone in to check. But it could have been the sunlight reflecting on a broken pane, couldn't it?

"What about the footsteps folks used to say they heard in the house?" Meredith couldn't stop herself from asking. "Do you know what that's about?"

"The house settling. Wind. Could be any number of things, right?"

Meredith supposed it could be.

"Now, you wanted to know about the Bufords?" Edna asked. Meredith liked this lady's no-nonsense style. "What about them?"

"What were they like?"

"They were…different." She pressed her lips together, making her look like she had no teeth.

"Different how?" Julia asked.

"They were just…" She hesitated. "Well, they kept to themselves for the most part. Weren't real friendly to outsiders. I really talked to Daisy the most, I suppose. She was nice enough. There was just… always something a bit off. Maybe it was all those kids, they plum wore her out. Maybe it was that husband of hers."

"Earl?"

"That's right." Edna had pulled a blue tufted pillow into her lap and was pulling at a loose thread. "He wasn't… Well, he was a drinker, I suppose."

"We know he got into some trouble over drugs," Meredith said.

"Yes, that too." She twined the thread around her finger.

"Do you know what happened to the family?" Julia asked. "Why they left?"

"Can't say I do," she said. "After Daisy passed, I didn't really keep tabs on the family. Wasn't really any reason to. Sometimes I'd hear a shotgun go off in the woods, or I'd see Earl headed up the river to head into town or to fish, but for the most part, no, they really kept to themselves. And then, of course, when the barn burned down, we all went out to help fight the fire. I remember hearing when one of the girls got married. Mellie? Nellie? Something like that. She was young. We all thought she must have been pregnant, but there was no baby. I suppose she must have just been looking for a way out of that place. Can't say I blame her."

"Wait. You said a barn burned down?"

"Sure. It was out by that field of flowers. You know." She nodded. She obviously thought she was communicating something that Meredith wasn't getting. "The flowers?"

Meredith still didn't get it, but Julia was already moving on.

"We've been inside the house," Julia said. "And from what we can tell, it looks like they must have left very quickly."

"Hmm." Edna pulled at the thread. "I don't know. Seemed like I heard things from over that way for a while before the county came in and took it over. I thought there were people living there for at least some of the time. But I couldn't say for sure. I remember when the county tried to sell the place for back taxes, but that was the first I'd known that they were all gone."

"Do you have any idea what might have made them leave?"

She shrugged. "Assumed it was probably the usual."

"The usual?" Julia raised an eyebrow.

"Money. Isn't it always about money?"

Was it always about money? A lot of things were. But was that what had driven the Buford family away?

"Do you think Earl owed someone money?"

"Possibly. Or maybe one of the kids did. There were a couple that seemed to get into trouble a lot, like their dad."

Financial trouble would line up with what the note in Earl's wallet indicated. "Do you know who they could have owed money to?"

"The county, for one." Edna laughed. "But aside from that, not really. Like I said, they kept to themselves, and I didn't really seek them out, if you know what I mean."

Meredith had one more question. "Do you know someone named Mario?"

"Mario?" She pressed her lips together again.

Just then the phone in the cradle next to the couch rang. Edna glanced at it and said, "That's my daughter, calling to check on me. She calls every day." She reached for the handset.

"We'll get going," Meredith said, pushing herself up.

"If you remember anything else about the Bufords, we'd appreciate it if you gave us a call," Julia said, slipping a business card from her purse onto the table.

"I will," Edna said. And then, into the phone, "Hello?"

Meredith and Julia thanked her again and saw themselves out.

"She's right about one thing," Julia said as they buckled themselves into the car again. "It always comes down to money, doesn't it?"

"Or drugs," Meredith said as she pulled out of the driveway.

"But that usually goes back to money too."

Meredith didn't really know all that much about the world of drugs, but she supposed that money probably did play a big part. But even with the cases she and Julia worked—the insurance frauds, the times they trailed a spouse suspected of cheating—it always did come back to who was set to lose what in a divorce or who was cheating whom out of what.

"Trust me. Some of the cases I heard…" Julia let her voice trail off and shook her head.

"Let's see what we can find out from the other neighbors," Meredith said. "Someone out here has to know something."

They drove to the next house Meredith had mapped out, a small wood-frame place tucked into the trees on a small rise. There was a car in the driveway, but no one answered when they knocked on the door. They also visited a well-cared-for double-wide trailer surrounded by neat landscaping, but there appeared to be no one home.

When they pulled up at the next address Meredith had found, a dog yanked against the rope that tied him to a tree and barked. Meredith climbed out uncertainly and stood before a battered single-wide trailer. The vinyl siding was peeling off and brown water stains edged the skirting, no doubt from the creek that ran just off to the left.

"Yeah?"

The door of the trailer opened, and a man stepped out onto the wooden porch. His stomach strained against the stained white tank top, and his baggy jeans were dirty. His buzz-cut hair was white, and his stubble matched.

"Hello. I'm Meredith Bellefontaine, and this is my friend Julia Foley." Meredith stepped forward and held out her hand. He glanced down at it and then shook it hesitantly. "We're trying to find out about the Buford family, who used to live a short ways from here. Did you, by any chance, know them?"

"Yeah." The word was slurred somehow, and Meredith realized he had a slug of tobacco in his cheek. "Used to come onto my land to hunt, even though it was posted."

"It sounds like you didn't get along with them," Julia said.

"Figured that out quick." He eyed them. "What do you want to know about them for? They been gone a long time. Left that house to rot."

"We're trying to find out why they left," Meredith said. "What happened that made them leave the house to rot."

"Hnh." He lifted his head, somewhere between a nod and a grunt. "I can't say I know for sure, but we all assumed something finally caught up with them."

"What kind of something?" Julia asked.

The man shrugged. "Figured it musta had something to do with those poppies they grew, but I don't know." And then, a moment later, he leveled his gaze at them and said, "Folks around here mind their own business."

Meredith looked at Julia, who was nodding. She had gotten the hint too.

"Thank you for your time." Meredith turned and walked down the steps, and as soon as Julia closed the car door, she backed out of the driveway. A spray of gravel shot up behind her as she pulled away.

"That was something else," Julia said.

"That was a waste of time," Meredith said. "Just like the others. How can it be possible that no one around here knows how an entire family just disappeared?"

"Someone knows what happened," Julia said. "They all knew the minute we showed up here this week. Someone knows where the Bufords went and why. They're just not saying."

"Then how do we get them to say?" Meredith asked. "We've only got one more house on my list, and it's the farthest away."

"I don't know how to get people to talk," Julia said, sounding as weary as Meredith felt.

"Why would they be keeping quiet in the first place?" Meredith asked. "What are they hiding? What are they protecting?"

Julia shook her head. "I don't know." She picked up Meredith's phone and typed in the address of the next house. "You're wrong, though."

"I'm wrong?"

"You said that visit was a waste of time. But it wasn't. We learned something important."

"What's that?" Meredith couldn't remember hearing anything that sounded like a clue or even a hint.

"I didn't pick it up at first, but I finally put it together. This guy told us they had poppies. A field of poppies," Julia said.

"Yeah?" Meredith didn't see where Julia was going with this. "They're pretty flowers."

"Do you know what poppies are used to make?" Julia had the map pulled up and set the phone on the dashboard.

"Poppy seed bagels?"

"Well, yes, that too, I suppose. But I was thinking of opium. Or heroin."

"Oh." Meredith couldn't believe she hadn't seen it before.

"Heroin is an opioid, and it comes from poppies. It's one of the biggest contributions to the opioid epidemic in our country today."

"Right." How had she missed that? "You'd need a lot of poppies, though, wouldn't you?"

"I imagine they must have had a large field. And the barn that burned? I'd put money on that being where they dried and processed the flowers."

"Wait. How does that work?"

"I'm not sure." Julia thought for a moment. "I'll call Beau. He'll know."

Meredith was going to say that she didn't need to do that, but Julia had already made the call.

"Hi there. How's the golfing today?"

Meredith couldn't hear Beau's response, but Julia nodded and then asked, "Hey, so Meredith and I want to know how to make heroin. Can I put you on SPEAKER?"

Before Beau could answer, Julia had changed it to speakerphone.

"Are you two getting into a whole different kind of business venture?" Beau asked, chuckling.

"Not today," Julia said. "We just heard that the family we're tracking was growing poppies. And we know the father was arrested on drug charges, plus we found drug paraphernalia in the house. And I know that heroin comes from poppies, right?"

"That's right," Beau said. "It's a hallucinogenic drug that's related to opium, and they're both made from the resin of poppy plants."

"How would you turn poppies into heroin or opium?" Meredith asked.

"I'm no expert, but I believe it would involve harvesting the liquid inside the plant and drying it out. Then probably heating it or something; I'd have to check on that."

"But you would probably do that in a large space, like a barn?" Julia asked.

"I would imagine," Beau said.

Meredith saw what she was getting at.

"Do you smoke opium? Like in a pipe?" Julia asked.

"Oh yes. Think of old pictures you've seen in museums. You've seen them there."

"Antique opium pipes can fetch quite a price at auctions," Meredith said.

Julia turned and narrowed her eyes at her. "How in the world do you know that?"

Meredith shrugged. "Ron used to go to flea markets and antique stores looking for items for his collections. You'd see them every now and then." The opium pipes she'd seen were most often decorative, with elaborately scrolled metal or richly painted enamel. But did that mean pipes used to smoke opium were always decorative? Could they possibly look more like the pipe they'd seen in the basement of the Buford house? She had no way of knowing. But thinking about that basement, Meredith had another question.

"You said opium is a hallucinogenic drug?"

"That's right," Beau answered. "Effects vary, but often opioids are used to numb pain and induce relaxation. But they can also have side effects. Opium is known for hallucinations."

"What are you getting at?" Julia asked, cocking her head.

"I'm wondering if that might explain why the basement was blocked off like that. Did Earl, or someone else in the family hallucinate something down there?"

"I see." Julia thought for a moment and then nodded. "Yes, I suppose that's a possibility. There's no way to really know for sure, but it could explain that."

"Should I assume you want to plant poppies in the garden next spring?" Beau asked with a laugh.

"I think I'll pass," Julia said. "But thank you for your help."

"Anytime."

Julia ended the call and turned back to Meredith. "So there you go. Poppies. If Earl was growing them, I think it's fair to say we now understand what he did for a living and why he kept getting caught with drugs in his possession."

"But all of the neighbors knew what they were up to. How did the authorities not know?"

"But like that last guy said, people keep to themselves around here. I suppose they just let them do their thing, as long as it didn't interfere with their own lives. And this place is basically a dense, largely uninhabited tropical jungle. Plants grow quickly here, and if the field of poppies was well off the beaten path, how would anyone have found it?

"It still doesn't explain what happened to the family," Julia said. "But it does help make the case that the disappearance was tied to drugs. A drug deal gone wrong, maybe."

"That's certainly the direction I think we should be focusing our attention," Meredith agreed.

As she steered toward the last house on the list, a text message popped up on her phone. She asked Julia to read it to her.

"It's from Lacey Marven," Julia said.

"Oh. Great."

"It says 'I found a few things you might be interested in hearing. Call me when you get a chance?'"

"I'll give her a call as soon as we get to the next house," Meredith said, following the directions on Julia's phone down another dirt road. "Lacey is the friend at the Effingham County Historical Society I told you about."

"Ooh. I wonder what she found."

"We'll find out soon enough," Meredith said.

They pulled up in front of the last house, a small wooden shotgun-style place, with a narrow front porch and battered siding. There were no cars in the driveway and no signs of movement.

"No one is home," Meredith said.

"I'll go and see, just to make sure." Julia climbed out of the car and walked up to door and knocked. Meredith stayed in the car and called Lacey. By the time Julia made it back to the car, shaking her head, Meredith was ready to go.

"Do you have time to make one more stop before we head back to Savannah?" Meredith asked.

Julia nodded. "Did you talk to Lacey?"

"I did indeed. And she has some interesting information for us."

Chapter Eleven

Willie,

The baby is kicking so much these days it's getting uncomfortable. I can't believe how big I've gotten, but the doctor says the baby is still healthy. Only a few weeks left. I wish I knew where you were.

Maybe it's silly to keep writing to you. I know you haven't gotten these letters because I know you haven't been at home for many months. Lou went back to your family's home today looking for you. I couldn't believe she had the guts, after the way they'd treated her last time, but she did. She told me she knocked right on that door and held her head high and demanded to know where you'd gone. She said a boy answered the door but not the same one as last time, so I guess it was Jed. She told him that you were about to become a father and she needed to know where you were. Well, apparently Jed then proceeded to say all kinds of bad things about me but then told her that you hadn't been around since May, after

123

you and your daddy had a big fight. I know you and your dad were always fighting, but I guess this one must have been really bad. So now I know why you're not writing back.

I miss you.

—R

The Effingham County Historical Society and Museum was housed in a red brick building just down the street from the courthouse Meredith had passed the other day. They parked in front of the building and met Lacey inside.

"Meredith! It's so good to see you!" Lacey pulled Meredith in for a hug.

"It's great to see you too." Meredith had always liked Lacey, and it was nice to see her here now. "This is my business partner, Julia Foley. Julia, Lacey Marven."

"It's wonderful to meet you," Lacey said. "Thank y'all for coming all the way out here." She ushered them past a small gallery, where Meredith glimpsed the words BETRAYAL AT EBENEZER CREEK on the wall, as well as several black-and-white photos of the now-familiar swampy creek. They went down the hall through a small lobby to a reception room with a fireplace and a few wingback chairs gathered around a wooden steamer trunk, which was used as a coffee table.

"We were actually nearby, so it wasn't very far out of our way at all," Julia said.

"Ah. You were out by the Buford place?" Lacey guessed.

"Talking to the neighbors," Meredith said. "Trying to find anyone who knew anything about what happened to the family."

"We're anxious to see what you've turned up," Julia said.

Lacey gestured for them to take a seat, and she sat across from them in one of the chairs.

"Well, I have to admit, there wasn't a whole lot of documentation about the family that I could find," Lacey said. "This branch of the Buford family doesn't appear in any church directories or baptismal records from the churches around here, and I wasn't able to find any number for them listed in a phone book. But we do have copies of some of the yearbooks from the high schools in the county. The collection is spotty, but I found one from Effingham County High School in 1985. There are four Bufords listed."

Meredith now saw that she had set the yearbook on the steamer trunk ahead of the meeting, and she gestured at it now. Meredith picked it up and started flipping through the thick glossy pages, yellowed around the ages.

"There's a Nathaniel Buford, who's part of the freshman class," Lacey said.

"Nathaniel?" Was that the name of the last Buford child? They already knew Eldan, Willie, Nellie, Laurel, and Jed.

"The thing is, he's listed in the baptismal records for St. Andrew's church, and his parents are listed as Hiram and Mary Buford," Lacey said.

"Hiram?" Meredith asked. Who was that?

"I looked him up, and Hiram's parents are listed as Frank and Martha Buford."

"So Hiram would be Earl's brother," Julia said.

"Which would make Nathaniel a cousin of the Buford kids we're looking for." Meredith looked down at the boy, who had brown hair with a cowlick and wore a checked short-sleeved shirt.

"There's an Eldan Buford in the sophomore class," Lacey said.

"He passed away a few years back," Meredith said.

"And Sadie Buford is also listed as part of the freshman class," Lacey said. She flipped to the right page. Meredith knew it was her the minute she saw her. She had the same reddish hair as the girl in the photo on Earl's dresser.

"That's the last Buford kid. The one whose name we didn't know," Meredith said.

"Is Sadie Buford listed anywhere else? Any other records?" Julia asked.

Meredith knew Julia needed facts to confirm what Meredith could already see.

"Not that I've found," Lacey said.

"This has to be the last daughter," Meredith said.

"She looks like she could be," Julia conceded.

Meredith pulled out her notebook and recorded the name in the family tree. That gave them one more name to go on.

"There's also a Willie Buford in the senior class," Lacey said.

Meredith didn't expect the twisting feeling in her gut at the sound of his name. After reading those despairing letters, she wasn't sure she wanted to see his face. But Julia flipped to the right page, and there he was. He had dark hair and a strong jaw that matched his father's, with a cocky smile. He was attractive, and he knew it.

Was Willie's son out there somewhere? Could he tell them what had happened to his father's family? How would they know how to find him?

"That was all I could find in the records we have here for this generation of the family," Lacey said. "I found several records for previous generations. But I haven't traced down anything else about this generation, at least on Earl's line. It seems like the family didn't have a lot of official ties to the community."

"Several people have told us that they kept to themselves," Julia said.

"I wonder if it was because of Earl's...business," Meredith said. "Better to fly under the radar."

"What was his business?" Lacey asked. "I also couldn't find any records that refer to what he did for a living."

"We believe he was growing poppies for the drug trade."

"Ah." Lacey nodded. "Opioids. Sure. That's plausible. There was just a big bust of a grower a few counties over last year. You don't hear of too many people growing that stuff these days, because it's so much easier and cheaper to import it from South America, from what I read. But there's a big problem with opioid abuse around here, and it wouldn't surprise me at all to find out people had been growing again, or that they'd been growing it back then. It's apparently big business. And it does make sense that you'd want to stay under the radar if your business was less than legal."

Meredith looked down at the new facts she'd recorded. They now knew the names of all six children, and she could go back to the archives and look for any information on Sadie and hope to get ahold of her. And they had the name Nathaniel, a cousin of the

Buford kids. If they could track him down, he might have some insight.

"Thank you for all of this," Meredith said, sighing as she closed her notebook. She really was grateful. Lacey had spent a lot of time looking through records and combing through the yearbooks. It just seemed that the more they found out, the less they really knew. She now knew the names of the children. It was a start, but it was only that. She needed more than names; she needed actual living people who were willing to talk about what they knew. She'd have to track them down.

"It was no problem," Lacey said. "But hold up." She put her hand up to stop Meredith from putting her notebook into her backpack. "You sent me Earl and Daisy's marriage license, and I saw that Daisy was from Guyton. It turns out her home address was on the same street where my grandparents lived when I was growing up."

"Really?" It wasn't that it was such an odd coincidence, really. Guyton wasn't a huge town—it couldn't be more than a thousand people these days, though it had probably been bigger when the railroad went through. It had a collection of beautiful historic homes that were listed on the National Registry of Historic places. It was more that she'd gotten the impression that Lacey was from a proud Southern family with, well, with a lot of money. And Daisy and Earl… The Bufords had had money once, that was clear, but she'd gotten the impression that they didn't really have a lot by the time Earl and Daisy were raising their family.

"My grandparents lived in that house for decades. It was sold off when they passed, but my mom grew up there, so I called her, and she knew Daisy."

"She did?" Julia's eyes widened.

"Daisy was a teenager when my mom was young, but she remembered her well."

"What did she say about her?" Meredith asked.

"Oh, according to Mama, Daisy was a proper Southern belle. Finishing school, cotillion, the whole works. I guess she was an only child, and her parents spoiled her something awful. And, I mean, I've seen the house she grew up in, obviously. It's in the historic district, and it's big. One of the biggest, with this beautiful wraparound porch and dripping in gingerbread trim. But Mama said Daisy was beautiful and so sweet, and everyone loved her."

"So how did she..." Julia let her voice trail off, but they all knew what she was going to say.

"Right. Well, apparently she met Earl at a luncheon at the DAR. He was working for the caterer, and they got to talking. And, well, give a sheltered girl a taste of excitement and a good-looking young man..." Lacey shrugged. "Her parents were apoplectic, of course. He was not at all the kind of man they had in mind for their daughter. But I've never seen parental disapproval serve to steer a headstrong young woman away from a man she thinks she's in love with."

"Forbidden love," Julia said.

"It's easy to believe things like class differences and money don't matter when you're young," Meredith said. She'd had one ill-conceived relationship with a college boy who set her heart racing even though they had almost nothing in common except attraction for the other. He'd been the first to realize that they had no future together and had broken it off with her—her first broken heart. But she remembered well the feeling that love could conquer all, despite all evidence to the contrary.

"They eloped," Lacey said. "Of course, once her parents found out, they insisted on a formal church wedding after the fact, but it seems everyone knew it was just for show. Willie was born seven months after the wedding."

"Did her parents cut her off?" Meredith asked. She'd heard of that happening when the parent didn't approve of a mate, though she couldn't for the life of her understand how a parent could cut off contact with a child.

"Not from what I understand," Lacey said. "My mom didn't think so. She said Daisy still came by sometimes, especially after the first baby was born. But then folks saw her less and less, and every time they saw her, she was looking a bit more ragged. Mama said they just didn't see her anymore after a while. She had heard that Daisy ended up having a bunch of kids and was living in squalor out there in the boonies with a moonshiner, and her parents just couldn't face it anymore. But who knows how much of that is true? Rumors have a way of evolving and growing." She shrugged. "In any case, that's what Mama knew."

Meredith tried to absorb this news. She realized she'd made some assumptions about Daisy without knowing anything about her, really. She certainly hadn't expected to hear that she'd been a blue blood who grew up having tea with the Daughters of the American Revolution. How had she gone from that upbringing to living in a swamp with a drug dealer? And did this new knowledge affect their assumptions about what had happened to the family? Meredith wasn't sure.

They chatted with Lacey for a while longer, and Lacey gave Meredith her mother's phone number in case she wanted to follow up, but Meredith was feeling more confused than ever by the time she got back to the car.

"We're getting closer," Julia said, but it sounded like she was trying to convince herself. "We've still got those family connections you reached out to. And don't forget Maggie Lu said she had something that might help. If we don't hear back from her soon, we can check in with her."

"She'll come through," Meredith said. She didn't know what Maggie Lu knew about the Buford family, but she did know that if Maggie Lu had given her word about something, she would deliver.

"You're right. And we'll figure this out," Julia said.

"I hope so."

Chapter Twelve

WHEN MEREDITH AND JULIA GOT back to the office, Carmen looked up from her computer and greeted them. "How did it go?"

"Let's just say we saw the full spectrum of humanity today," Julia said.

"Oh, it wasn't that bad." Meredith stood for a moment, enjoying the cool, air-conditioned air inside the lobby.

"I thought that guy in the tank top was going to bring out a shotgun," Julia said. "But we learned a few things. Poppies, for one."

"Poppies?" Carmen narrowed her eyes.

"For heroin." Meredith nodded.

Carmen slowly nodded, as if this all made perfect sense. Meredith was about to explain, when Julia jumped in. "How was everything here?"

"The phone was ringing like crazy today." Carmen handed them each a stack of phone message slips. "You two are in demand."

"Oh dear." Julia looked through the stack of slips and sighed. "That husband really wants an update on Isabella," she said.

"He said he had a meeting with his lawyer coming up," Carmen said.

"I still don't have any proof," Julia said. "I probably need to spend some time focusing on that this afternoon."

Meredith had other work to do, but none of it was a rush. And she couldn't get the image of that abandoned house out of her head and couldn't stop wondering what kind of terror or tragedy had driven the family to flee, leaving all their treasures behind. But it was cases like the worker's comp one that paid the bills. "I'll spend some time on the insurance fraud case this afternoon," Meredith said. She flipped through the rest of the messages. There were a couple of inquiries about their rates, which she'd pass off to Carmen to answer, and one connection she'd reached out to in one of her background check cases, and...wait.

"That last one seemed kind of confused about why exactly you were getting in touch with her, but she said you'd sent her an email. She's connected to the Bufords somehow?" Carmen shrugged. "Anyway, she left her phone number there if you want to call her back."

It was from AnnaMae Harrington. She was the second cousin of the Bufords Meredith had found on the genealogy site. She felt her heartbeat speed up. Was this it? Was this the connection that would bring this whole mystery into focus? Someone out there had to know the answers to their questions. Maybe it was AnnaMae.

"I'll give her a call right now," Meredith said, and followed Julia down the hall. Julia headed into her own office while Meredith tossed her purse down on the chair and sat down behind her desk. She dialed the number on the slip of paper and held her breath while it rang.

"Hello?" The woman who answered the phone sounded winded, and there was a baby crying in the background on her end of the line.

"Hi, this is Meredith Bellefontaine. I'm calling for AnnaMae Harrington."

"Oh, hi. You're the one who emailed about the Buford family, right?"

"That's right," Meredith said. "I was so pleased to get your message."

"Hey, I'm sorry, but I've got to run out and pick my kid up from soccer practice. Can I give you a call later? Or, wait, you're in Savannah, right?"

"That's right. Right near Forsyth Park."

"I'll be down that way tomorrow for a haircut. Maybe I could talk to you then?" The wailing from the baby in the background grew louder.

"It would be wonderful if you wanted to come to our office to meet. Or I could take you out to coffee or something if you'd rather."

"That's great. My appointment should be over by two. Just text me where to meet, and I'll see you there."

"I will. Thank you—"

But before she could get the next word out, the line went dead. Ah, well. AnnaMae had her hands full. Meredith remembered those days, back when it had felt like just getting through the day was a major victory. Her boys had been born ten years apart, so she'd hauled Chase to plenty of Carter's soccer practices and karate lessons and T-ball games. Those days were exhausting. And yet she sometimes missed them so much her heart ached.

Next, she called Nellie Corporon again but got no answer.

"I need to head out." Julia appeared in the doorway, her bag slung over her shoulder. "Apparently Isabella didn't show up at her Pilates class, so I need to find out where she's gone instead." She hitched her bag up. "I went to college for this."

"And law school, don't forget."

"How could I forget? I'm almost finished paying off those student loans."

"Have fun."

"You too," Julia said. "Don't stay here too long."

"I plan to work on the workers' comp case," Meredith said. "But then I have to head home. Quin is taking me out to dinner."

"Ooh! Have fun."

After Julia headed out, Meredith returned a few phone calls, and then she turned to the photos she'd taken on her phone of Aaron, looking for anything that would indicate he didn't really have a debilitating back injury. But there was nothing there. Nothing to show one way or another if he was lying about his back injury preventing him from work. She needed to find a way to nail this guy, to catch him in the act. She'd drive past his place on the way home and see if there was any new evidence. But there was one more thing she could do before she left for the night.

Meredith already had the photo app open on her phone, so she flipped through the pictures she'd taken of Ron's golf clubs, as well as his coin collection. She wouldn't be working on the guest room tonight, but she could upload the photos she'd taken and list them on eBay to sell them. She'd asked Julia if Beau wanted them, but he was content with the set he had. She'd bought a few things on eBay in the past, and it couldn't be that hard to figure out how to sell things.

Twenty minutes later, there they were. The golf clubs that had once been sitting under her Christmas tree with a big red bow, now listed for sale online. She still remembered how wide Ron's smile had been when he'd seen them and how he'd kissed her right then and there. He had been out on the golf course two days later, and he came home laughing and kissed her again. Seeing those clubs now, listed for sale, should have given her a sense of peace, knowing that they would soon be making someone else laugh and smile, and they'd be out of her guest room to boot. She felt tears sting her eyes.

"*Adiós.*" Carmen appeared in the doorway of her office and froze. "I'm sorry... I—"

"No, I'm sorry, Carmen." Meredith took a tissue from the box and used it to dab the corners of her eyes.

"I thought you were working on insurance fraud, or I would never have—"

"I know. It's okay." Meredith crumpled up the tissue and tried to laugh. "It's silly. I decided I'd just take a few minutes and list a couple of things for sale online before I headed home."

Carmen's brow wrinkled, and Meredith realized that made no sense on its own. She needed to explain.

"Ron's things. I just listed Ron's golf clubs for sale on eBay, and I just…" She took in a deep breath and fought the tears that threatened. "I didn't expect…"

"It's okay," Carmen said. She stepped into the office and came around the desk so she could see the screen. "Those are nice clubs."

Meredith pressed her lips together and nodded.

"Why are you selling them?"

Meredith turned away from the screen and waited a moment, and then she said, "It's time. They're just taking up space in the spare room. They might as well go to someone who can use them."

Meredith reached for another tissue and wiped away the tears that had spilled over as she spoke.

Carmen watched her for a moment, and then she tilted her head and said, quietly, "They're not taking up *that* much space, are they?"

Meredith didn't know how to answer. She focused on blinking back tears and dabbing at the ones that didn't stay where they were supposed to.

"Maybe hang on to them a bit longer," Carmen said, shrugging.

Meredith nodded, and Carmen leaned over and hugged her, an awkward chair hug, before turning back toward the door.

"I'll see you tomorrow," Carmen said and then walked out, leaving Meredith alone. Meredith sat still, staring at the screen, remembering how long Ron had spent researching which set of clubs he'd wanted. He'd studied several golf magazines, and spent hours in the sporting goods store, trying them out, and finally landed on this set.

She didn't need these golf clubs. It made no sense for her to hang on to them. They were just taking up space, and it would be better to let them go so someone else could use them. But she reached out and gripped the mouse, and, before she could change her mind, she clicked the button to cancel the sale.

She wasn't ready.

***

Quin picked Meredith up in his red Land Rover and drove her to her favorite Italian restaurant right near the river. It had dark wood paneling and red-and-white checkered tablecloths and white candles held up by wine bottles and the best pizza in Savannah, in Meredith's opinion.

"So," Quin said, sliding onto the bench across from her in the wooden booth. He wore pressed khakis and a blue polo shirt, and he looked relaxed and comfortable. "How did your trip to visit the neighbors go today?"

Meredith had told him what she and Julia were planning to do this morning, and he'd cautioned her to be careful.

"It was...well. It was interesting." Meredith told him about the older woman in the log cabin, and the man who'd told them about the poppies. And she told him about what they'd learned about Daisy from Lacey at the Effingham County Historical Society. A waitress brought water and sweet tea for Meredith, and they ordered the Mama Rosa's pie, which was topped with fresh mozzarella, spinach, marinated artichokes, and a creamy sauce. It didn't sound like it would taste good, but it was delicious.

"It seems like Daisy lived to regret her decision to marry Earl," Quin said.

"I don't know." Meredith took a sip of her tea and set it down. "She never left him, anyway."

"How could she leave? She had six kids. Was she going to leave them behind or take all of them with her?"

"She could have taken them to her parents," Meredith said. "Her family had means. Surely she could have gone to them if she'd really needed out."

"Maybe her parents wouldn't help. A 'you made your bed now lie in it' situation."

"Maybe. I guess it's hard to say how other people feel. On the outside, it seems like she took a step down. But I guess she must have loved him."

"I'm sure she did. But that doesn't mean it was easy to be married to him, with all those kids. You said they didn't interact much with the world outside? Or have many connections with society?"

"They didn't seem to," Meredith conceded. "And I would guess that once the honeymoon period passed and the reality of what her husband did for a living set in, it was hard to bear. But I don't know if I can say she regretted it, necessarily."

"Fair enough." Quin smiled. "I suppose that she loved those children, no matter how hard life got, and wouldn't have gone back and redone things if it meant not having them."

Meredith nodded and then waited. It sure sounded as if he was saying more than he was really saying, and she let the silence stretch out to encourage him to speak. But when he didn't go on, she said, "How is Jamie?"

"She's doing great. Her birthday was last week, so we talked for a while. Grace is loving preschool. She is going to be Elsa for Halloween."

"That will be really cute," Meredith said. "And I'm glad Jamie's doing well."

"I am too." Quin used the straw to stir the water around in his glass, swirling the ice. "I'm...well, to be honest, there were times when she didn't have a great example of a strong marriage to look up to, so it's really encouraging to see how she and Jason have built such a solid relationship."

Meredith wanted to know more but sensed she had to tread carefully here. "I suppose every marriage has its rough patches."

"Yes, that's true. But I'm afraid our rough patch lasted for much of her childhood. I was working all the time, trying to build my career, and Andrea was left alone with Jamie much of the time. She asked me to help out more, to be present more, but I felt like I couldn't, not with the type of job I had at a big firm, not if I wanted to make partner someday."

Meredith knew Quin had been a successful contracts attorney back in Atlanta, and he still practiced law here in Savannah, but not for a big firm. These days he made his own hours and worked the schedule he wanted.

"Looking back now, I realize that I could have made a number of different choices that would have made things better. But at the time…" He let his voice trail off. "We had this big house, right on the golf course. I thought I needed things like that to impress my colleagues, and of course that meant I had to work even more to pay the mortgage. Andrea kept telling me we didn't need a big house and fancy cars, but I couldn't see it at the time."

"It sounds like you understand now," Meredith said.

"I do, but I almost lost everything in the process," Quin said. "There was a period of time there where… Well, Andrea and I hardly saw each other, and when we did interact, we were fighting. I was seriously considering divorce." He shook his head, keeping his eyes down. Meredith couldn't read the look on his face. Was it pain? Guilt?

"But you didn't leave."

"I did, for a while. A couple of months. It was awful. I was crashing with a guy from work, living in his guest room, staying up too late and drinking too much. I missed them so much, but I couldn't bring myself to admit that I'd made a mistake."

"What brought you back?"

"Prayer," he said softly. "Andrea never stopped praying for our marriage, and eventually the Lord started to work on my heart too." He took a sip of his water, and then continued. "Andrea deserves all the credit for the fact that our marriage survived that period. She never stopped fighting for our marriage, and she never stopped praying for it either. I came back home, and we started going to counseling, and I started going to church with them more regularly, and, well." He shrugged. "We decided we wanted our marriage to make it."

"And you did make it," Meredith said. She knew Andrea had died just a few years back and that she and Quin had been married for many decades at the time. She and Ron had been married for more than forty years when he passed. They'd had rough patches too, as any married couple did, she supposed. She'd loved him, even in the rough times, but it hadn't always been easy.

"We did, with a lot of counseling and a lot of prayer. And I'm so grateful. But looking back now, I can't help but think of the things I missed because I was wrapped up in my work. When I think about how much of Jamie's childhood I just wasn't there for…"

"The way you talk about her, she seems to have grown into a wonderful adult just the same," Meredith said.

"She really did. And Andrea deserves all the credit for that too."

Just then, the waitress brought the pizza, setting it down on a metal stand on the table between them. Once she left, Quin blessed the food and said, "Anyway, I'm sorry. I didn't mean to burden you with all that. I was just trying to say that I bet Daisy didn't have it easy, but even then she wouldn't have traded it despite that."

"I'm sure you're right," Meredith said but then found that she couldn't say more. Something about the vulnerable way he'd shared about his own marriage, coupled with the grief she'd unexpectedly felt when she had tried to list Ron's golf clubs for sale, left her flummoxed now.

"Hey." Quin reached across the table and touched the back of her hand. "Are you all right?"

Meredith nodded, because she couldn't say more just yet. Each couple's marriage was different, and it was impossible to say what it was like inside the relationship. She and Ron had had their ups and downs, but she'd loved him till the day he died. She hadn't thought that she would ever get over the grief of losing that relationship. And she hadn't, if today's meltdown was any evidence. But her grief had softened, lost its hard edges. Losing Ron didn't feel as unbearable as it once had. She might not be ready to give up all of Ron's things yet, because that felt like losing a part of him. But she was starting to see that there could be happiness in a life beyond Ron. She'd never stop loving him and never stop missing him, she knew that. She'd never *not* be Ron's wife.

But these days, sometimes, she could even imagine finding romance again. Not anytime soon. But with the right person... She looked across the table and saw Quin watching her, biting his bottom lip.

"I'm just glad to be here with you," she said. It didn't come anywhere close to what she was feeling, but for the moment, it was enough.

November 30, 1985

Willie,

I'm having contractions more regularly now. I've been having them for a few days, but they're more steady now. I think the baby is coming soon. I hope you get to meet him.

 —R

MEREDITH WAS JUST SETTING DOWN her purse Friday morning when Julia appeared in the doorway of her office. "Maggie Lu called. She asked us to come by the library this morning."

"When?"

"She didn't say." But Julia didn't move, and Meredith knew what she was thinking by the way she was hovering. "Let me just scan my email, and we'll go. Give me ten minutes?"

Twenty minutes later, the women were walking up the steps of the Carnegie Library, Meredith clutching a travel mug of the coffee she would normally have sipped at her desk. They entered the brick building and looked around. The place was quiet on this Friday morning, but there were a few patrons using the computer terminals and a few mothers with young children in the reading area. They found Maggie Lu crouched down among the stacks of children's books, shelving colorful picture books. Meredith saw the title of the one in her hand just before she slid it in. *Jabari Jumps.*

"Hello there." Maggie Lu smiled up at them, set the last book in its place on the shelf, and used the metal shelving unit to pull herself up. Meredith held out her hand, but Maggie Lu ignored it and raised herself to standing. "How are you ladies this morning?"

"We're just fine. How are you doing?"

"Oh, I'm all right." Maggie Lu put her hand on the cart that was loaded down with beautiful books. "It didn't take you ladies long to get here."

"As soon as I got your call, I insisted we come first thing," Julia said.

"She didn't even let me drink my coffee," Meredith confirmed, holding up the thermos.

"Sorry not sorry." Julia grinned at her.

"Well, it sounds like I better leave these books for later and show you all what I found."

"That would be great," Meredith said.

Maggie Lu turned and, gesturing for them to follow her, walked away from the children's section to the reference desk. Maggie Lu walked slowly but with a regal grace and a straight spine that Meredith wished she could mimic. Maggie Lu sat down behind the reference desk and gestured for them to sit in the two chairs across from it.

"So. Julia told me you were interested in the Buford family." Maggie Lu made a sound at the back of her throat that indicated dislike.

"That's right," Meredith confirmed. "And you knew them."

"I didn't know them well," she said. "But I did interact with some of them back in 1985."

"You were helping a young woman find Willie, the father of her baby," Meredith said. "We read about it in her letters."

"That's right," Maggie Lu said. "I first met her when I was gathering signatures to erect a memorial to the people who were drowned in that river. You know about that?"

"We do," Meredith confirmed. "It was a terrible thing."

"You got that right." Maggie Lu took a deep breath and let it out slowly before she continued. "Well, I was part of a group that was campaigning to get a monument put up, and I was assigned to get signatures from residents in the area. So I go out to that swamp and start knocking on doors."

"You did that by yourself?" Meredith remembered some of the neighbors they'd met in the area and couldn't imagine it was at all safe for a woman to go out there alone back then.

"Who else was going to do it?" Maggie Lu asked with a shrug. "Anyway, I went up to this one house, this big old plantation-style place that had seen better days, and met a man at the door. When I asked for his signature… Well, he wasn't interested, he made that clear."

Meredith didn't even want to imagine what he'd said to her.

"I had no interest in sticking around, so I left. It was time to head home, so I walked to the bus stop closest to the house and I ran into a young woman. She was clearly pregnant, and she told me she'd seen the man chew me out. She said she was sorry and that he had a temper. We got to talking, and I found out that one of the young men who lived in the house was the father of her baby."

"Willie," Julia said.

"That's right." Maggie Lu nodded. "She told me Willie wouldn't talk to her or acknowledge the pregnancy. She also told me she hadn't been to a doctor and wasn't sure when the baby was due. She said she lived with her father, and he drank a lot and hit her sometimes. She had an older brother who had left several years before."

"You got all that while you were waiting for the bus?"

"You ever tried taking public transportation out that way?"

Meredith and Julia both shook their heads.

"Let's just say you don't do it if you have any other options."

The way she said it made Meredith think it was probably an understatement. She knew Maggie Lu had never learned to drive, and she supposed this girl was unable to have a car for one reason or another.

"Well, anyway, I felt bad for her. She seemed young. I mean, she was young, obviously, just a teenager. When she got off the bus I asked her for her phone number so I could check in on her, and she gave it to me. I couldn't get her out of my head, so I called her a week later and told her I was going to see that she got to the clinic."

"It sounded in the letter like her father didn't want her to see a doctor."

"Didn't want to pay for it, more like. He preferred to drink his paycheck away." Again, that noise at the back of her throat that indicate dislike. "Charlene and I drove out to her place and picked her up. It was this horrible trailer. Rusty sides, broken steps, overgrown yard littered with car parts and who knows what all."

As much as Meredith was enjoying the story, she wished Maggie Lu would cut to the chase and tell her what happened. But she knew better than to rush her.

"Inside was even worse," Maggie Lu continued. "It was filthy, just packed with stuff and covered in dust and I don't know what. And it was hot. Stifling. There was no air-conditioning, and it was only June. I didn't see how she was going to make it through the summer there as she got bigger.

"We took her to the free clinic in Springfield, and the doctors said the baby was healthy. That made her happy. I held her hand as she listened to the baby's heartbeat. It was wonderful, but I felt sad for her. It seemed like she really had no one else."

"She was trying to find the baby's father," Julia said. "She was writing him letters because she couldn't find him any other way."

"I know she was," Maggie Lu said. "And I wanted to help, but I didn't. Not at first. I was busy myself, with my job and trying to get signatures for that memorial. Plus I was in the choir at church, and they did not mess around. You did not miss practices for that."

The way she said it made Meredith laugh. She did not doubt that choir practice was mandatory at Maggie Lu's church.

"I checked in on her, though, and when it got to be July, I brought her an old window unit air conditioner because I couldn't bear the thought of her without one."

"That was kind," Meredith said.

Maggie Lu shrugged. "You've been pregnant. You know what it's like."

She did indeed. Those had been some of the hardest months of her life.

"She called me late one night, oh, around the middle of August, and told me she was bleeding. Charlene and I went and picked her up and took her to the emergency room, and the doctor said she had to stay on bed rest."

"She mentioned that in a letter," Meredith said. "Placenta previa." Meredith had had a similar scare when she was pregnant with Chase. The doctors had thought the placenta would prevent the baby from being born naturally and was likely to pull loose from her uterus altogether, but it had resolved itself within a few weeks and she hadn't needed to go on bed rest herself.

"I don't know what it was called, but she ended up lying in bed for the rest of those months, going out of her mind with boredom. Even after the problem with the placenta cleared up, she had some other kind of complication that meant she was flat on her back all the way through. So we brought her books and food a few times."

"That was kind," Julia said.

"It was the decent thing to do. I'm telling you, this girl had no one looking out for her. I met her dad once. He was a drunk. The mom had died a few years back. It was a terrible situation. And she was really sweet.

"She was still writing these hopeless letters to the baby's father, hoping he would respond, but I could see that he wasn't going to. At first I thought he was just ignoring her, but then I started to wonder if he might not be getting them."

"Hadn't the people at the Buford house said Willie wasn't there?" Julia asked.

"Yes, and they said the same thing whenever Ruby called, but she didn't know whether to believe her at first or not."

"Ruby," Meredith said quietly. R stood for Ruby. "That was her name?"

"Ruby Haywood," Maggie Lu said. "That was her."

Meredith jotted the name down and then gestured for Maggie Lu to continue.

"As time went on and her letters went unanswered, I think she started to realize that he wasn't getting them. She didn't know where he was or how to get in touch with him, and she was stuck there in that bedroom in that horrible home. That's when I volunteered to find him myself."

"She wrote in the letters that you looked for him in prisons and in hospitals."

"Jail was the first place I looked. Based on what I'd seen of the family, that seemed like a good bet. But there was no record of him in any prison in the nearby counties. That's when I checked the hospitals. I even went to the county office to look up death records and court cases, but he didn't show up there either."

Meredith didn't know when Maggie Lu had found the time among all her other responsibilities, including her own two children. It really had been an act of Christian generosity, she could see.

"Then I went down to the army recruiting station to see if he'd enlisted," Maggie Lu said. "That seemed like a good way to disappear. But they didn't have any record of him, and neither did the navy or the air force or the coast guard. That's when I went back to the house and demanded answers. I told them that Willie was about to become a father, and even if he didn't have the decency to do the right thing and step up and support his pregnant girlfriend and their child, at the very least he should acknowledge the child and not just pretend it didn't exist."

"She wrote about that in her letters," Meredith said. "She said you talked to one of the boys."

"It wasn't the one I'd met before," Maggie Lu said.

"It was Jed," Meredith said.

"He was just as unpleasant as his father and his brother," Maggie Lu said. "But I could see the news was a surprise to him. He hadn't known Willie was about to have a baby. He told me there had been a big fight, and Willie hadn't been around since May. That's when we knew for sure Willie hadn't gotten the letters."

"So he didn't know about the pregnancy," Julia said.

"We were pretty sure he did not," Maggie Lu said. "Of course, that just made me all the more sure I was going to find him."

"Did you?" Ruby's letters had ended without an answer or any more information on what had happened to her or the baby. "Was the baby born? Was he okay?"

"What happened?" Julia asked.

Maggie Lu continued with her story as if she hadn't heard their questions.

"A funny thing happened when I was walking back to that same bus stop where I met Ruby. I heard footsteps behind me, and when I turned I saw a girl running after me. One of the sisters, I assumed."

"What color hair did she have?" Julia asked.

"Red."

"Sadie," Meredith said. Julia nodded.

"Well, Sadie, if that's who she was, told me she'd overheard my conversation with her brother and she was sure Willie didn't know about the baby. None of them had seen or heard from him since he'd left."

"So he just, what, vanished?" Julia asked. "And his family didn't feel the need to look for him or find out where he had gone?"

"It didn't make sense to me either," Maggie Lu said. "That would never happen in my community. But I had already figured out that these people were very different from me. And I got the sense that they were…well, it was clear something dramatic had happened. It wasn't just a small fight that had sent him packing. That was clear in the way they all talked about it. I later found out that Willie had accidentally set a barn on fire. That was apparently a big problem, and his father let him have it."

Meredith processed this. So Willie had set the barn fire that they'd heard about. If the barn had truly been the place where the poppies had been dried and processed, she imagined more than just the barn went up in flames. The family's inventory would have burned up as well. Which would have meant a huge loss of profit. Was that how they had ended up unable to pay their tax bill?

But also—Maggie Lu had found that out later. Which meant she or Ruby had had further contact with the family at some point. How? What had happened?

"What else did Sadie say?" Julia asked. "Did she follow you all that way just to tell you about the fight? Hadn't Jed already done that?"

"That's right," Maggie Lu said. "She didn't just tell me that. She followed me to tell me to look for him down at the docks. She'd heard through a friend that Willie had gotten a job on one of the commercial fishing boats down at the harbor."

The harbor was one the main ports in the state, and all kinds of ships ran in and out of it.

"And did you?"

"You better believe I did," Maggie Lu said. "I marched right on down there as soon as I could. It wasn't until a few days later, and Ruby was having serious labor pains by then, so I knew time was of the essence."

"I wouldn't even know where to start down there," Meredith said. She hadn't spent a lot of time down at that part of the waterfront.

"I didn't either," Maggie Lu said. "And let me tell you, the whole place smelled like fish and was coated in a slimy layer of who knows what. I don't see how people could stand it. But I held my nose and marched up to the first fisherman I saw."

Meredith wanted to laugh. Prim, proper Maggie Lu surrounded by raw fish.

"I talked to one fisherman who didn't know him. He directed me to another, who thought the description I gave sounded familiar, but he thought Willie was on one of the deep-water boats that was out at sea. No one could tell me for sure when it was coming back. So I left and came back the next day, and the boat was back."

"And was he on it?"

"Yes, ma'am. I asked for a Willie Buford, and when he showed up, he was just like Ruby had described him. I told him that he had better leave those fish behind and come with me because he was about to become a father."

"How did he respond to that?"

"He stammered a bit, and then he followed. We took his car and went straight to Ruby's place, and she was in the early stages of labor. I recognized it immediately, so I asked Willie to take her right to the hospital."

"Wow." Meredith tried to imagine what it must have been like for Willie to find out he was becoming a father and then become one all in the same day. "Was Ruby glad to see him?"

"She cried. 'Course, that could have been because of the pain, but I don't think so."

Meredith thought about those plaintive letters, longing for Willie to respond. She couldn't imagine what it must have been like to finally see him again after all those months.

"The baby was born the next morning. Willie was there when Lyle was born."

"Lyle," Julia said.

"Lyle Haywood." Meredith wrote the name down.

"He was a handsome baby," Maggie Lu said. "With lots of hair and a loud cry."

"You met him?" Julia asked.

"After all that? You better believe I did."

"Where is she?" Meredith asked. "How is she? How did it all turn out?"

"I don't know," Maggie Lu said. "I'm sorry to say I lost touch with Ruby a long time ago. She eventually got married—not to Willie, though I believe he was present in Lyle's life—and moved away, and I don't know what happened to her after that."

Meredith looked over at Julia. She could see that Julia was pleased to hear that Maggie Lu had tracked down Willie, just like she was.

"Here is what I wanted to show you," Maggie Lu said, pulling an envelope out of the pocket of her coat. "Ruby sent me this picture a few years after the baby was born. That's Willie there. Took me a few days to dig this out, but I knew you'd want to see him."

Meredith leaned forward and studied the photograph. Willie looked older than he had in his yearbook photo, hardened somehow. But he still had that strikingly handsome face, and he was looking down at the little boy with clear tenderness.

"Is Willie still alive?"

"I don't know," Maggie Lu said. "That was the only time I ever met him."

Meredith had hoped for more, but she understood. And there were still several things that didn't make sense to her.

"How did the letters from Ruby end up in Willie's mother's bedside table?" Julia asked.

Maggie Lu shrugged. "I imagine she must have kept them."

"Right." Julia laughed. "What I meant was, why? Why would she keep them—you said this was in 1985, right?"

Maggie Lu nodded.

"She died the next year," Julia said. "But why would she keep those letters if she wasn't even in touch with her son?"

"It was her grandchild," Meredith said simply. "Maybe her first." Meredith had kept the scrap of paper she'd been doodling on when Carter and Sherri Lynn had told her they were going to have a baby. She'd kept every photograph, every card, every memento she could from each of her grandchildren. They were some of her most precious possessions. "If these letters were all she had to know that child by, I'm not at all surprised she would have kept them."

Maggie Lu nodded along.

"This means that Willie didn't vanish with the rest of the family when they fled the house," Julia said. "Willie was already gone by the time the others left. Were there other Buford children that were gone by that point too?"

Meredith realized she was right. "I don't know."

There were so many things they didn't know. They still didn't know what had driven the family away or what had happened to Willie and Ruby and the baby. They didn't know where the other siblings were or whether any of them were still alive.

But they did know two new things. "We now have two more names to go on," Meredith said.

"People who were intimately connected with Willie Buford," Julia added.

"The phone books are just over there," Maggie Lu said, pointing to the shelf just off to her left. "And the research terminals are right over that way," she added, a knowing smile on her face.

***

The Carnegie Library had phone books for not only Savannah, but also for Effingham, Bryan, Bulloch, and Liberty counties, and after combing through all the pages, they came up with a list of three Lyle Haywoods and one Ruby Haywood. They called each, but only got through to one man named Lyle, who was far too old to be the Lyle they were looking for. They left messages with the others, and then they spent a few minutes searching through the newspaper archives for any mentions of either of them, but with no results. Meredith wanted to stick around and keep searching, but she knew they had to get back to the office. AnneMae Harrington was due to stop by in less than half an hour. They'd texted this morning and she'd agreed to meet at the office.

"Let me know if you find out any more names," Maggie Lu said as they headed out the door. "And I'll see if I can dig up any information about them."

Back at the office, Carmen handed Meredith a message. Meredith looked down and saw that it was from Marco Corporon. That had to be someone related to Nellie.

"They called back!" Meredith shrieked. Their luck was finally turning. Another person intimately connected with the Bufords, and in the same day.

"Yeah, but read that message," Carmen said with a knowing look.

"He says to stop calling. His mother does not have any good memories of her family, and she does not want to talk to us about them," Julia said while reading over Meredith's shoulder. "None? She has zero good memories? That's crazy."

"It seems unlikely." Meredith let out a sigh. "But the response is pretty clear." She thought for a moment. "But why? And why does no one want to talk to us about them?"

"Let's call him and find out." Julia was already reaching for the phone on Carmen's desk. "Should I?"

"That seems like a bad idea," Carmen said.

"The message is pretty unambiguous," Meredith added.

"What's the worst he can do? Hang up on us?" Julia was already dialing the number from the slip of paper.

File a restraining order, for one, Meredith thought, but bit her tongue.

"Hello?" The man's voice came out through speakerphone.

"Hi there. Is this Marco Corporon?"

"Yeah."

"This is Julia Foley, from Magnolia Investigations, and I wondered—"

"I thought I told you people to leave our family alone," Marco said. "I do not have anything to tell you about my grandparents or their rat trap of a home, and my mother has no wish to talk about her past."

"Why did they leave?" Julia asked quickly.

"My mom left because she couldn't stand to be among a bunch of druggies and idiots anymore. She ran off and married the first guy who would get her out of there, and he turned out to be not much better than the people she left behind. As for the rest of them, I don't know. Once my grandmother died, there was nothing good left in that house. My mother did not maintain contact with her family after that, and I believe it was for very good reason. Now, please, leave her alone."

The line went dead.

"Well then," Julia said, pressing the button to disconnect line one. The dial tone went silent. "I guess that settles that."

"But at least we know how Nellie felt about her family," Meredith said.

"And her husband," Carmen added. "It sounds like she was so desperate to get out of there that she married a dud."

She wouldn't have been the first girl to marry for a way to get out of her parents' home, but it always made Meredith sad to think about.

"And it sounds like any little thread of relationship that was there was with Daisy," Julia said. "And once she was gone..."

"What a tragedy." Meredith shook her head.

"But is it a clue?" Julia asked.

Meredith couldn't help the grimace she made, and Julia waved it away. "Look, okay, I know it sounds heartless, but listen. We already know Nellie wasn't the only one who went away because the situation at home wasn't what it should have been," Julia said. "Willie left for what sounds like the same reason."

"What are you getting at?" Meredith asked.

"It's horrible to contemplate, I know, but it sounds like something wasn't right out there in that house."

"Are you suggesting Earl…"

Meredith couldn't even bring herself to say it.

"I'm not suggesting anything. Just asking, why is no one willing to talk about what went on in that house, and what if Nellie and Willie weren't the only ones to leave because of it?"

Before Meredith could figure out how to respond, the door opened, and a woman with bottle-blond hair stepped into the lobby. She wore fitted white capri pants and wedge shoes and a big smile.

"Hi." She looked around at each of their faces. "I'm AnnaMae Harrington."

"Hello!" Meredith stepped forward and shook her hand. "I'm Meredith Bellefontaine. Thank you so much for coming."

"And I'm Julia Foley. We're so glad you're here." Julia also shook her hand.

"I have to admit, I'm curious about your research project," AnnaMae said. She looked around at the lobby. "What a gorgeous office. And in such a perfect location too. How magical to be right on such a lovely square."

"We are very lucky," Julia said. "It's a great space."

"Why don't we head back into my office?" Meredith suggested, and led them down the hallway and ushered their guest into one of the chairs across from her desk. AnnaMae remarked over the fireplace and the antique trumpet before she sat down in a chair.

"I saw that you had quite an extensive family tree built on the site," Meredith said as they settled in. "You must be very into genealogy."

"I find it fascinating," AnnaMae said. "And, well, now that the kids are more independent, I have more time, so I got pretty deep into it. My friends play tennis or collect antiques." She shrugged. "I research my family's history."

"Have you found anything very surprising?" Julia leaned forward to ask.

"Oh sure. I found a census record that showed my grandfather was married to a woman I knew as Aunt Elinor growing up." AnnaMae laughed. "She was a family friend and she was at all the family gatherings, and I guess she was married to my grandfather before my grandma was. No one ever talked about it, but it seems they all got along. I don't know. Both of my grandparents are gone, so I can't ask them about it, but yeah, I guess that happened."

"Wow." Julia's eyes were wide. "I cannot imagine."

"I can't either," AnnaMae said. "But you always find interesting things when you look into the past. They were people, just like you and me."

"I couldn't agree more," Meredith said. She had a feeling that she would get along with AnnaMae if they met socially. She always liked people who valued history.

"So," AnnaMae said. "You're interested in the Buford family, is that right?"

"That's right," Meredith said. "I think Daisy Buford was your... second cousin?"

"That's right. Aunt Daisy was my mother's cousin. She wasn't really my aunt, we just called her that out of respect."

"That makes sense," Julia said. That kind of thing wasn't uncommon in these parts. A child couldn't exactly call an adult by their first name, so there were a lot of aunts and uncles who were not really aunts and uncles. "Did you know the family well?"

"I don't know that I'd say well," AnnaMae said. "We used to go over there sometimes for holiday gatherings when I was a kid."

Meredith did some quick math. She guessed AnnaMae was probably a kid in the seventies and early eighties, around the same time as the Buford children.

"What was it like?" Meredith asked.

"Oh, it was fun," AnnaMae said. "There were always so many kids there. Not just the six Bufords, but Uncle Earl's brothers and sisters would bring their families over, and it was just a fun time. We'd play in the creek and build forts and I don't know what all." She shook her head. "There was this big field of the most beautiful flowers." She laughed. "I guess I know why he'd get mad when we picked them now. When I was a kid I had no clue why it would matter that we'd picked a few flowers when there were so many."

"So you knew about the poppies," Meredith said.

"I only put it together much later," AnnaMae admitted. "But when I figured it out, it did help explain why we stopped going to see them."

"What do you mean?"

"Oh just that, as things started to unravel there, we went there less and less."

"Unravel how?"

"Well, keep in mind, I was probably in junior high at the time, so my memories are kind of fuzzy. But Uncle Earl had started acting kind of...erratic, I guess you'd say. He was caught with drugs a few times, and...well, the kids were getting older and were starting to get in trouble, and the house just started to feel kind of...dumpy, I guess. Like, things would break and they wouldn't fix them. The big spreads at holidays got smaller. You got the sense money was tight, though of course you'd never speak of such things."

"Do you remember the last time you were there?" Julia asked.

"Oh yes. I'll never forget it, probably. My little brother Robbie— he was probably only four or five at the time—had found a loaded pistol in the library and was playing with it. My mother started screaming at Earl about having loaded firearms where kids could get to them, and he told her there were loaded guns in every room in the house, to keep the family secure. Well, my mama was never one to hold her tongue, especially when she was riled up, and after that scare, she didn't hold back. Said he wouldn't need to be afraid for his family if he got a respectable job and stopped dealing with bad people and all kinds of things that I didn't understand at the time. We weren't invited back after that."

"Goodness. A loaded gun in every room of the house?" Meredith couldn't believe it, not with that many children around.

"He was paranoid, clearly, but maybe he had a right to be, given the type of people he was hanging out with."

"Have you kept in touch with any of your cousins?"

"No." AnnaMae shook her head. "My mama wanted to go for Daisy's funeral, but my daddy didn't want to run into Earl, so we didn't go, and I just... Well, we were never all that close to begin with."

"Do you know why they left the house?" Meredith asked.

"I'm sure they all left for different reasons," AnnaMae said. "And then the county took it."

"Right," Julia said. "The older ones were gone, sure. But before the county took the house, back when at least some of the kids were still living there, the family abandoned it, quite suddenly, judging by the state of how things were left. Do you know why that was? Did someone threaten them?"

AnnaMae's head was tilted. "I don't know. I was always under the impression they just couldn't afford the house. I don't know of any event that made them all leave suddenly."

"It seems pretty clear that they didn't have time to gather their things or clean up before they left," Julia said.

"Huh." AnnaMae seemed stunned. "I never heard that."

"Do you know how to get in touch with any of them?" Julia asked.

"I don't know. I'm not sure if Mama knew. Maybe she had addresses for some of them? I can look. But I don't know."

It sounded like the family had splintered quite dramatically.

"Do you know of anyone named Mario?" Meredith asked.

AnnaMae thought for a minute and then shook her head. "Sorry. It doesn't sound familiar. Who is it?"

"That's what we're trying to figure out." Meredith sighed.

"One more question," Julia said. "We've heard rumors that the house was haunted—"

"Oh sure." AnnaMae was nodding. "Definitely."

"Wait. What?" Julia's wide eyes reflected the shock that Meredith felt too. Everyone else they'd spoken to so far had denied it. "What makes you say that?"

"You would always hear footsteps in a room where no one was," AnnaMae said. "Or doors would mysteriously open and close. Windows too."

"Could it have been a draft?" Meredith asked.

"Once or twice, sure. But it happened all the time. The kids would laugh about it. Like, 'oh, there goes Eloise again.'"

"Eloise?" Julia asked.

"Some long-dead ancestor who had apparently been accidentally shot on the property a hundred years ago or something."

"Not surprising if they kept loaded guns in every room of the house," Julia muttered.

"So, you experienced things that made you believe what they said was real?" Meredith was still trying to make sure she was hearing this right.

"Oh, sure. I know there are people who say ghosts aren't real, but trust me, I spent enough time in that house to know they're wrong."

Chapter Fourteen

AFTER ANNAMAE LEFT, JULIA AND Meredith sat in Meredith's office, talking over what she'd told them.

"I believe that she experienced things she couldn't explain at the time," Julia conceded. "But it was just the house settling or a rush of wind or something."

"There has to be a logical explanation," Meredith agreed.

"Let's focus on what we did learn," Julia said. "We found out that someone close to the family is not aware of any major event that drove them off. It was just running out of money, according to her."

"But it sounds like she wasn't in close contact with the family by that point. Would she have really known?"

"I don't know." Julia sighed.

"We still need to see what we can find out about Sadie and Jed Buford, and Ruby and Lyle Haywood," Meredith said. "Maybe one of those contacts will give us more information."

"We've already been to the library once today," Julia said. "Maybe we could ask Maggie Lu to see if she can find out anything about them."

"It can't hurt to ask."

"I need to grab lunch and head out to tail Isabella to make sure she goes to her hair appointment like she's supposed to. And then I need to take off a bit early. Beau got tickets to the opera. I swear that man could watch *Madame Butterfly* every night and never get tired of it."

Julia pretended opera was Beau's thing, but Meredith happened to know that she enjoyed it quite a bit herself.

"Enjoy. You deserve a night out."

Julia thanked her. "And don't you work too hard," she warned Meredith.

"I won't. I need to call this insurance company back," Meredith said. "And then I'll give Maggie Lu a call."

"All right," Julia said, and pushed herself up. "We are getting closer, you know."

"It sure doesn't feel like it," Meredith said.

"We are. I can feel it."

Meredith shook her head.

When Julia went back to her office, Meredith decided it was a good time to do some recon on Aaron's case. She'd camp out in front of his house for a while this afternoon. Maybe she could do some research while she was waiting. But first, she had another call to make.

"Carnegie Library, this is Rebecca. How may I help you?"

"Oh, hello, Rebecca." Meredith had met the resource librarian many times and found her to be helpful and kind. "This is Meredith Bellefontaine. I was looking for Maggie Lu. Is she available?"

"Hi, Meredith. Let me see if I can find her." Rebecca placed her on hold, and a minute or two later, Maggie Lu picked up and said, "You missed me already?"

Meredith laughed. "We always miss you, Maggie Lu. But I was wondering if you had time to do some research for us."

"If it's about the Buford family, you'd better believe I do."

"Thank you. We'd like to see if there are any records on the children named Sadie and Jedediah."

"Want me to see if I can find anything more about Ruby and Lyle Haywood while I'm at it?"

"Have I ever mentioned how much we appreciate you?"

Maggie Lu laughed. "I can always hear it again."

"We love you, Maggie Lu."

"Anything else?"

Meredith was about to say no, but then she thought for a moment and said, "We're also looking for someone named Mario."

"Mario?"

"I think it's a first name," Meredith said. "Though I'm sure that doesn't help much."

"What's the context?" Maggie Lu sounded skeptical.

"It was in a note we found in Earl Buford's wallet," Meredith said. "It said, 'Bring the money to Mario's by midnight Saturday. He'll be waiting.' We figured Mario was someone he owed money to, but we haven't been able to figure out who it is."

"Mario's?"

There was something strange in Maggie Lu's voice. "What?"

"You are sure that's a person?"

"No. I don't know. Why?"

"Used to be a nightclub by that name on Montgomery, just over the border of Martin Luther King Boulevard. I'd pass it all the time."

"Huh. What was it like?"

Maggie Lu snorted. "I wouldn't have gone inside even if I could have. So I don't know. I just remember it being a neighborhood eyesore, and lots of folks trying to get it shut down."

"It sounds like it could have been the sort of place where Earl might have gone," Meredith said.

"It does indeed." Maggie Lu made a noise at the back of her throat. "I don't remember when it finally closed down. But I can look into it."

"That would be wonderful. Thank you."

Meredith hung up, and she spent a few minutes answering emails before she pushed herself up. She needed to find proof for that worker's comp fraud case.

"I'm headed out," she called to Carmen, who nodded and waved without taking her eyes from the computer screen.

Meredith grabbed a sandwich from the Corner Café, a little shop selling sandwiches and coffee, before climbing into her car and driving back to Wayne Street. She parked at the end of the block, where hopefully the neighbor she'd spoken to before wouldn't see her. Aaron's car was parked in front of the house again, but she didn't know if he was inside or not. She would sit and wait.

While Meredith waited, she used her phone to browse social media profiles for men named Lyle Haywood. The first she found was the young rector of a small church in Plymouth, England. Probably not the right man, she decided. There was a high school track star in Florida, a man who wrote pithy tweets from Duluth, and a man who owned a clock repair shop in Savannah.

Meredith clicked on that profile. The picture showed a man in his late thirties, she guessed, with curly brown hair. Two small girls sat in his lap, and a woman she guessed was his wife sat next to him. The page wasn't used very often, but he was tagged in a few posts by someone named Ruby Stone. Well now, that was interesting.

This was the right Lyle. It had to be. She felt excitement course through her veins as she opened up the message tab and started typing. She was just about done typing out a request to meet up when movement out in front of Aaron's house caught her attention. It was Aaron, Braves cap on his head, a big black garbage bag slung over his back. Meredith fumbled with her phone, trying to close the message and open her camera app, but before she got it open, Aaron had tossed the bag onto the sidewalk in front of the house. She heard something metal inside clink against the cement.

That was it! He was fine! He had just tossed that bag and turned around and wandered back into the house with no problems. That was her chance to capture proof that Aaron was fine, and she had missed it. She waited, hoping he would come out with another bag, but there didn't seem to be any more.

She banged her head against the steering wheel. It was so stupid. How could she have forgotten why she was here and what she needed to be paying attention to?

Meredith let out a sigh. She needed to come up with a better plan.

***

Meredith successfully sorted through two boxes of Ron's clothes that evening, and she had just finished bringing them to the living room so she could load them into her car when the doorbell rang.

She set the last box down by the door and looked out the peephole. Maggie Lu.

"Hi," Meredith said. She tried to keep the surprise out of her voice. "Please, come in."

"I hope you don't mind me coming over. I found something interesting, and I wanted to tell you about it right away."

"Of course. I'm so glad you're here." She ushered Maggie Lu inside. "Can I get you a drink?"

"No, I'm all right," Maggie Lu said.

"Have a seat." Meredith gestured toward the overstuffed chair in the living room. "How did you get here?" It sounded like a strange question, but Maggie Lu didn't drive, and this was quite a distance from the library and her own home.

"The bus runs right here. It was no trouble."

Meredith didn't believe it was no trouble, but she had to admit she was anxious to hear what was so important that Maggie Lu felt she had to come over instead of just call.

"I told you about a place called Mario's that used to be over on Montgomery." Maggie Lu leaned forward and pulled a manila folder out of the boxy leather purse at her feet. Her linen skirt somehow looked elegant, even after a full day of wear. "I did some research into it today, and I found something interesting."

She opened the manila folder and pulled out photocopies of newspaper articles. Meredith could tell by the fonts and layout that they were old, but it wasn't until Maggie Lu handed over the articles and Meredith looked at the top of the page that she saw the first article was from the July 18, 1989, issue of the *Savannah Morning News*.

"Read it." Maggie Lu gestured at the page.

Shooting at Nightclub Injures Three

Police responded to a call reporting shots fired at Mario's Nightclub at 11:23 last night. Three people were seriously injured and transported to Candler Hospital. Their condition remains unknown. The skirmish reportedly broke out when two men began arguing over money, and the suspect brandished his weapon and began making threats toward one of the victims. Two other patrons tried to intervene, and the suspect, who remains in custody, fired at the three men.

Mario's has been the site of several violent incidents in the past decade. In 1983, a man was fatally shot after a disagreement, and in 1986, a man was fatally stabbed. Witnesses reported that incident revolved around a drug deal gone wrong.

Police did not make any comment regarding last night's events, stating that the incident was still under investigation.

"Wow. Sounds like a heck of a place."

Maggie Lu shook her head. "Not the kind of place where I would enjoy spending time. But keep reading."

Meredith saw that the next article in the pile was from the following day's paper.

Nightclub Shooting Victim Dies; Two More Remain in Serious Condition

One of the victims of Monday night's shooting at Mario's Nightclub was declared dead at 3:16 yesterday afternoon, after a surgery failed to repair major damage to an artery.

*The victim has not been identified, pending the family's noti-
fication. The other two victims remain in serious condition.*

*Details have been slow to emerge, but a witness, who
wished to remain anonymous, said that the disagreement
involved a payment for drugs.*

The next page in the stack was an article from October 17, 1986,
reporting on the stabbing incident. And the next page was a piece
about the 1983 shooting. The details were sketchy in both pieces.

"Drugs seems to be a common theme in this case so far,"
Meredith said. "But how does this relate to the Bufords? They'd
already lost the house to the county by 1989, so they were long gone
from the area."

"Were they, though?" Maggie Lu cocked her head.

"Wait. Are you saying they weren't?"

"I honestly don't know how that house ended up the way you all
found it. I'm just saying that you two have been so certain that the
family all fled in one dramatic moment that you haven't been able to
see other possibilities."

"Possibilities like what?" What else, besides a great threat, could
cause them to leave in the middle of breakfast, with a dress laid out?
What else could cause Earl to leave so suddenly he would forget to
take his wallet? So many of the family's treasures were there. What
else besides an imminent threat could have caused them to leave
them all behind?

Maggie Lu was hinting at something in line with what Anna-
Mae had suggested earlier, but Meredith just couldn't see it. Nothing
else made sense.

"You're the detectives here. I'm just pointing out that you've got tunnel vision. And if you keep reading, I think you'll understand why I believe that."

Meredith obediently turned the page and found a follow-up article to the 1989 shooting that indicated that a second victim of the shooting had passed away in the hospital, and then, following that, a police investigation into the management of Mario's. Shortly afterward, the bar was closed temporarily, and then, two weeks later, it was announced that the place had been permanently closed. Police had uncovered a drug ring operating from the bar and were investigating how far and wide it ran.

"It sounds like the city was better off for that place being closed," Meredith said.

"Oh yes." Maggie Lu nodded. "Without a doubt."

"So is that the connection? Earl's trips to Savannah were about selling his heroin through Mario's, and once it closed, he was out of luck?"

"I don't know for sure but would guess you got the first part right," Maggie Lu said. "Judging by the note you found in his wallet. But as you've already pointed out, the county owned the Buford house and land by the time Mario's was shut down. So I don't think Earl's business could be hurt by the closure of Mario's."

Meredith flipped the page of the last article, but there were no more papers in the stack.

"So what is it?" Meredith asked. She could feel herself growing more frustrated by the moment. "What does all this tell us?"

"I can't say for sure that it tells us anything, besides telling us that the place found on that scrap of paper in Earl's wallet was notorious as a place for buying and selling drugs," Maggie Lu said. "But we know that Earl was involved in drugs. And we have him connected to Mario's, based on that note you found. And according to that note, he owed someone money, and that person wanted it badly enough to make a threat. And we know that there were several fatal incidents at Mario's over the years, which all seem to have involved money for drugs."

She looked at Meredith over the rim of her glasses, watching her, waiting for her to put the pieces together. Meredith could see the retired schoolteacher in her; instead of telling Meredith what she was thinking, Maggie Lu was going to make her figure it out herself.

Meredith ran through all of the fragments of facts in her mind trying to see what Maggie Lu was getting at.

"Do we know who the victims were in those other cases?" Meredith asked.

Maggie Lu was nodding now. "I was not able to find that reported in the papers. But I believe it is worth trying to find that out."

"Earl couldn't have been the victim in the 1983 shooting," Meredith said. "Because we know he was alive in 1985, when you visited the Buford house."

"That's right."

"But we don't have any record of him after 1985," Meredith said. She was starting to see what Maggie Lu was suggesting. She thought Earl might have been the victim in the 1986 stabbing.

"But there was no death certificate for him."

"There was no death certificate for him in *Effingham County*," Maggie Lu clarified. "If—and that's a big if—*if* he was involved in the 1986 incident, well, a death certificate would have been issued in Chatham County, would it not?"

It hit her then. "So it was Earl who was stabbed in 1986?"

"I don't know." Maggie Lu was shaking her head. "It's nothing more than a guess, really. But if it was, it could explain a few things."

It would explain more than a few things, Meredith thought. They would know what had happened to Earl, but beyond that, it would mean that both Earl and Daisy were gone a year before the county repossessed the house and land. If it was just the children left in that house...

"Don't get too far ahead of yourself," Maggie Lu cautioned. "But if it were me, I'd be down at the county clerk's office first thing in the morning, trying to find out if Earl Buford's name is listed in the records."

"Thank you, Maggie Lu."

"The only catch is that you have to tell me what you find."

"Of course."

Maggie Lu sat still and looked around the room, and she looked in the direction of the boxes Meredith had brought down. "Doing some cleaning?"

"Those are Ron's things," Meredith explained, but Maggie Lu nodded. She'd already figured that out, clearly.

"I couldn't face it for years after Darwin died," Maggie Lu said. "I thought I could, after the first year, but when I started to think about getting rid of his things, well..." She let her voice trail off. "I wasn't ready."

"It's been two years for me," Meredith said. "And I thought I was ready, but, well..." She gestured toward the boxes.

Maggie Lu didn't say anything for a moment. She bobbed her head slightly, almost nodding, but not quite. And then, finally, she said, "Grief takes time. You can't rush it. It's okay to wait."

Meredith felt tears sting her eyes, and though she had been so certain she wanted to get Ron's things out of her house, now she wondered if she needed to take the advice of a woman who had been through this too. Meredith just didn't know.

Chapter Fifteen

MEREDITH WAS WOKEN BY THE phone ringing Saturday morning. She glanced at the screen. Julia.

"Hello?"

"I got her!"

"Who?" Meredith's mind was still in dreamland.

"Isabella. She was cheating! I got a clear shot of her making out with her Pilates instructor last night."

"Oh." Meredith glanced at the clock. It was just after eight. "That's great, I guess?"

"I mean, it's not great, it's terrible. It's horrible that she's cheating, and it means she won't get any money in the divorce. But still, I got proof. How awesome is that?"

Meredith needed some coffee before she could be as excited as Julia was. "It's great news," Meredith said. Now they would get their full fee. But she didn't see why this couldn't have waited an hour. "Is that all?"

"Did I wake you?"

Meredith let out a sigh. "I should probably get up anyway."

"Sorry, I didn't realize what time it was. I've been up for hours. But you should go back to sleep. We'll talk more later."

And with that, Julia hung up the phone, and Meredith lay back against her pillow. She could try to go back to sleep, but she doubted she would be successful. She might as well get up. She pushed herself out of bed and started the coffee.

Meredith hadn't been planning to work on Saturday; she'd hoped to spend the day tending to her garden and making cinnamon rolls for coffee hour at church. But after she ate breakfast and did her devotions, she poured herself another cup of coffee and looked at her social media accounts. To her delight, there was a message from Lyle Haywood, Ruby Haywood and Willie Buford's child.

Mrs. Bellefontaine,

I'm not sure I can tell you much about my biological father, but I can tell you what I know, and my mom might be able help. She works with me in the shop Saturdays, so if you want to stop by sometime this afternoon, we might be able to help.

—Lyle

And then he gave the address for the shop Time After Time in Savannah.

That was interesting. She was sure she could work that into her day. Then she checked the website for the Savannah County Clerk's office. She wanted to check out Maggie Lu's hunch and see if there was a death certificate for Earl on file in Chatham County. She was disappointed to discover that the records weren't available online. However, just as she was about click off the site, she noticed something. The office was open on Saturday morning, from nine to noon.

Well then. Begonias forgotten, Meredith got dressed and drove toward the county clerk's office, at the courthouse. For such a beautiful city, Meredith couldn't understand how Savannah had ended up with a hulking modern mass of cement for a courthouse, but there it was, on Montgomery Street. The parking lot was mostly empty, and the halls were quiet when Meredith stepped inside. On the second floor, she found the clerk's office, and when she announced she was interested in searching old death records, the woman at the desk clapped her hands. It was an odd response, Meredith thought, but she supposed the woman was probably just glad for something to do. There was no one else here.

"Just have a seat at one of the computers," she said, coming around from behind the desk. She was thin, with purple streaks in her hair, and she had to be in her early twenties at the most. She wore a ring that went from one nostril to the other.

"The records have mostly been digitized," she said, waking Meredith's computer. "It can be a bit spotty, especially the farther back you go. If you don't find what you're looking for, let me know and I'll see if I can find it in some of the files in the back."

"Thank you," Meredith said, and allowed the woman to show her how to log into the search system. She wore rings on every finger, Meredith noticed as she opened the database. Meredith was so curious about who she was, but she knew she needed to focus.

"Now, if you want a copy of anything, we do charge ten cents a copy for that."

"Thank you."

Meredith waited until the woman had gone back to her desk and then typed the name EARL BUFORD into the search window. She hit RETURN, and...

There it was. Earl Walter Buford, dead on October 17, 1986. She clicked on the name, and the system pulled up a digitized copy of the death certificate. Earl had been pronounced dead at Candler Hospital at 1:24 in the morning. The cause of death was listed as *hemorrhage from laceration*. Bleeding to death from a wound, in other words.

It wasn't proof, exactly, but it was pretty close. A man had been stabbed in Mario's on October 17, 1986, over a disagreement about drugs. He had been taken to Candler Hospital and pronounced dead. Earl had been involved in drugs and had been ordered to deliver money to Mario's; he had also died on October 17, 1986, of a laceration.

It seemed obvious that Earl was the man who had died, but without corroborating evidence, it wouldn't hold up in court. Meredith knew that a good lawyer would declare it all circumstantial evidence, since it wasn't actual proof that the man stabbed that night was indeed Earl.

But this time around, she wasn't worried about whether a case would hold up in court. She was only worried about finding out the truth. And she knew, without a doubt, she'd found it.

Meredith whipped out her phone and called Julia. "I found Earl," she said. The noise brought her a disdainful look from the girl at the desk, who pointed to a sign that said PLEASE NO PHONE CALLS stapled to the front of the desk.

Meredith mouthed "sorry" and gathered up her things. "Hold on," she said into the phone and then thanked the woman before heading out into the hallway.

"You found Earl? Where?" Julia was saying.

"He died in 1986 in a knife fight at Mario's." Meredith proceeded to tell Julia what Maggie Lu had shared and how she'd discovered his death certificate.

"Wait. Hold up," Julia said. "But if he died in 1986, does that mean the rest of the family ran away after he died? Were they still facing some kind of threat?"

"Maybe," Meredith said. "I mean, we don't know for sure that he was the only one involved in the drug trade. It's possible one or more of the kids was involved as well. Aren't these things often family businesses?"

"More than you'd expect," Julia admitted.

"But here's the thing. Maggie Lu said we've had tunnel vision, assuming the family all got up and left because of some traumatic event that caused them to leave in the middle of breakfast and never look back."

"Yeah, because that's what it sure seems like, based on what we found inside that house," Julia said.

"It certainly did. But what if that's just the story we believed because it was the most obvious? What if assuming that caused us to miss some other story the house was trying to tell us?"

"First it's ghosts, now you think the house is speaking to us?"

"Not literally. Just, you know, what if we read it all wrong?"

"How? What is the alternative story the house is telling us now?"

Meredith hesitated. "I don't know yet. But I think we need to go back there and check it out again."

"When?" Julia let out a sigh. "Beau and I are supposed to go to a barbecue tonight at the house of one of his golf buddies, but I'm free until four or so."

Meredith was about to say "now," but then she remembered the message from Lyle Haywood. She needed to go to his shop this afternoon.

"Oh my goodness. I didn't tell you about the message I got from Ruby's son."

"What?"

Meredith told her how she'd searched social media and found what she'd thought was the right Lyle Haywood and sent him a message the day before.

"And he wants you to stop by to talk to him and his mother this afternoon? His mother, the woman who wrote those letters to Willie?"

"That's the one."

Julia was quiet for a moment and then said, "So when are we leaving?"

***

Lyle had invited her to stop by Time After Time Saturday afternoon, and it was officially past noon when Meredith and Julia stepped inside the small storefront on Broughton Street. The sign on the window read Horology and Clock Repair. Meredith did not know what horology was, but she understood that it was a clock shop. The walls featured old-fashioned pendulum clocks and cuckoo clocks and modern round-faced clocks, while the display case showed various watches, pocket watches, and mantel clocks. There was even a section of tide clocks, which Meredith imagined must be useful if you lived right on the coast.

"Hello." The woman who greeted them couldn't be Ruby, Meredith thought. She was too young, with curly long hair, still a dark rich brown, fanning out around her shoulders. She wore stylish jeans and boots, and she had a soft, soothing voice. Was Ruby here somewhere? "How can I help you?"

"My name is Meredith Bellcfontaine," Meredith said.

"And I'm Julia Foley." Julia held out her hand.

"I'm looking for Lyle Haywood," Meredith said. "I contacted him with a question about his family."

"Oh, that's right. Lyle said you'd be coming by today. I'm Tamar, Lyle's sister." She slipped off the stool where she'd been sitting and shook their hands. "It's nice to meet you. Hang on."

She vanished into the back, and Meredith noticed the quiet but constant ticking that echoed throughout the shop.

A few moments later, a man came in from the back with a magnifying glass over one eye. He pushed it up when he saw them, and then he smiled.

"Hi. You're the one who sent me a message about my father," Lyle said. He had a round face and a neatly trimmed beard, plus the same dark hair as his sister.

"That's right. I'm Meredith." They introduced themselves again, and Lyle gestured for them to step over toward the side of the shop.

"I can't tell you a lot about my biological father," Lyle said, shaking his head. "I was a kid when he passed away, and I didn't know him all that well."

It was the first Meredith had heard that Willie had passed away, and the news hit her harder than she would have expected.

"We're looking into what happened with his family and their house," Julia said.

"Oh, that old place." Lyle shook his head again. "Even when I was a kid, that place was falling down. I used to think it was so creepy. I hated going there."

"Did you spend much time there?" Meredith asked.

"Not a lot. My grandparents died when I was really young, so I don't even remember them, but my dad took me there once so I could see 'the old home place,' as he called it, when I was about four or five. The family didn't own it anymore by that point, and it was boarded up, so we never went inside."

"Then your father was in your life?" Julia asked.

Lyle shrugged. "I mean, sure. Kind of. I saw him a few times a year until he died. He always brought me a present, like he thought that made up for not being around. My dad—the man I think of as my dad—was Mitch, the guy my mom married when I was eight."

"My father," Tamar called from the other side of the store.

"Once Mitch was in the picture, Willie kind of faded, and then he moved to California and passed away, and that was kind of that," Lyle said.

"What was Willie doing in California?" Meredith asked.

"Trying to be a movie star, from what I hear." Lyle shrugged again. "Waiting tables, mostly."

It was clear from his tone of voice how little he felt for his biological father. Meredith was sad, thinking about how cavalier Lyle was about his father's death, though she couldn't really blame him for that. It just made her sad to think what Willie missed out on by not being more involved in his child's life.

"Did you get to know any other members of the Buford family?" Julia asked.

"I keep in touch with—"

"Hi there!" A woman bustled in the door of the shop wearing a long, flowing dress. "I'm sorry I'm late. I got caught up with giving Max a bath."

Meredith assumed Max was a dog, but it wasn't totally clear.

"That's fine. Mom, this is the woman I mentioned who asked about Dad." Lyle gestured to Meredith, and she held out her hand.

"I'm Meredith Bellefontaine. And this is Julia Foley."

"Ruby Stone."

Even though she'd known she would be here, Meredith still felt herself start. After reading her plaintive letters, hearing her desperation grow in her words, it was strange to see her standing here live in front of her. Her dark hair was threaded with gray, her features delicate and her skin pale, and her eyes were tired but kind.

"I'm not sure how much I can tell you about Willie and his family, but I'm happy to tell you what I know."

"Thank you so much," Meredith said. "But before we start, I think these belong to you."

Meredith reached into her purse and pulled out the stack of letters they'd taken from the house and handed them to Ruby. Ruby looked down, flipping through the few at the top of the stack. Meredith knew the moment she'd figured out what they were; in a rush, tears filled her eyes and ran down her cheeks.

"Oh my," she said. "Oh my."

Meredith watched Lyle and Tamar, who had frozen, unsure of what do. Meredith was pretty sure she wasn't unhappy, just overcome, but she couldn't be sure.

"Where did you get these?" she asked quietly.

"We found them in Daisy Buford's bedside table," Julia said.

"She kept them?" Ruby tilted her head.

"She kept them along with her Bible and other things that were precious to her," Meredith said.

"What are those, Mom?" Lyle came up beside her and peered down.

Ruby didn't answer for a moment; she stood with her eyes closed and held the letters close to her chest. The ticking of the hundreds of clocks seemed to grow louder in the silence that stretched out. Then, quietly, she said, "These are the letters I wrote to your father to tell him I was pregnant. He finally came to meet you when you were born, because of the kindness of a wonderful woman who tracked him down for me." She stopped and took a breath and then continued. "I assumed the family had tossed the letters away as they came in. It never occurred to me that she would have kept them."

"We don't know why she kept them," Julia said softly, "but we assume it was because they were how she learned about her first grandchild. And no matter what else was going on in that family, we guessed that she loved that child."

"She came once, to meet him," Ruby said, eyes shining. "She and Willie were not on speaking terms by that point. And she and I had never gotten along. She didn't approve of the way Willie was living his life, and I suppose I was seen as a part of that. But she wanted to meet Lyle, so she came to my father's home, where I was living, and brought a blanket she had made."

"That blue crocheted one?" Lyle asked.

Ruby nodded. "She also sent a check when he was born." She set the letters down gently on the counter. "Thank you for these."

"I'm glad they were appreciated," Meredith said.

"So what do you want to know about the Bufords?" Ruby asked.

"We're trying to figure out why the family abandoned the house," Meredith said.

"Well, I don't know anything about that. I can tell you why Willie left, but I don't know about the rest of them."

"Maybe you could start at the beginning," Julia said. "When did you first meet them?"

"Willie and I went to the same high school," Ruby said. "Well, it was the only one in the county back then, so everyone went there. I lived way out in the northern part of the county, so I'd never crossed paths with the family until he sat down next to me in algebra."

"Romantic," Julia said, and again, they all laughed.

"Isn't it though?" Ruby shook her head. "He was a senior, and I was a sophomore, and he was struggling, so I offered to tutor him."

"A classic move," Tamar said.

"What can I say? He was older and very good-looking, and I was...well, let's just say I wasn't getting a lot of love and support at home. You know where this leads."

"Did you get to know the rest of the family while you were... dating?" Meredith asked.

"Dating is a kind way to say it," Ruby said. "I realized later that Willie was 'dating' other girls as well. But at the time, I thought he was the most wonderful catch, and I thought I was the luckiest girl in the world. He was a handsome bad boy, and I thought I could be the one to tame him. I was a walking cliché." She glanced over at her two children on the other side of the shop. "I'm grateful that my own children are smarter than I was and made better decisions."

"We had the advantage of a great dad," Tamar said.

Ruby nodded. "Mitch was pretty wonderful."

Meredith took that to mean her husband had passed away, and she felt a wave of compassion for this woman, who had already been through so much. With the constant ticking of the clocks, it was impossible to not think about the passing of time, how they were inexorably moving forward, moment by moment, and the past was behind them all, just out of reach.

Julia stayed focused on their goal. "You said you knew why Willie left the family home. Can you tell us about that?"

Ruby nodded. "After he graduated—in no small part due to my help at algebra, I'll have you know—his father wanted him to come work at the family business full time."

"The family business being…"

"The poppies," Ruby confirmed. "They grew that huge field of poppies and harvested the gum inside in that big drying shed, and then they'd process it and Earl would run it down to Savannah at night. There was a lot of work involved, and it had gotten to the point where Earl wanted someone stationed at the field to guard it day and night. All of the kids helped out with that to some degree, but he didn't pay them much, and Willie thought he could make more by getting another job. And then, when he dropped some ash that hadn't extinguished, and the barn went up, well…I guess Willie's father brought out one of his many guns."

Meredith cringed, imagining the scene.

"I only found out about it after the fact, after Lyle was born. I'd finally broken up with Willie when I found out he'd been seeing other girls, and that was before I knew I was pregnant. I didn't realize Willie had left home and joined a commercial fishing rig and wasn't getting my messages. I called and wrote letters and showed up in person trying to let him know about the baby, but no one told me he didn't live there anymore. It was just like he'd vanished. But someone helped me track him down."

"Maggie Lu," Meredith said.

Ruby cocked her head.

"Otherwise known as Louvenia, or just Lou," Julia said. "We know her. She has fond memories of you."

"Oh wow." Ruby took a deep breath. "My goodness. What an amazing woman. I don't think she'll ever know how much she helped me."

"We can put you in touch with her, if you'd like to thank her yourself," Julia said.

Ruby nodded. "I would like that very much."

"We'll get that to you before we leave," Meredith said. And then, leading the discussion back to Willie, she asked, "So, did Earl really point a gun at his son?"

Ruby nodded again. "He fired it too. He didn't hit him, of course. I think he meant to just scare him, but all it did was drive Willie further away."

"What was the rest of the family like?" Meredith asked.

"Eldan was a bully. He was used to getting his way. I didn't see Jed around too much, but Sadie was kind. She talked to me and treated me kindly. Nellie was standoffish. Willie avoided his father, and so did I. And Daisy just seemed overwhelmed. She spent a lot of time in her room, sleeping mostly, as far as I could tell. The few times I saw her, I got the impression she was bewildered by how her life had turned out the way it had. But again, she spent so much time by herself that I don't really know."

"Sounds like depression," Meredith said. She was no medical expert, but this wasn't hard to pick up on. And after the loss of a child, it wasn't all that surprising.

"Or some kind of medical condition," Ruby said.

"Or just raising six kids while being married to a drug lord," Julia added.

Whatever the case, it sounded like Daisy had a rough time of it toward the end.

"Did you ever hear that the house was haunted?" Meredith asked.

Ruby laughed. "There were rumors, but I don't know. I always suspected the flashing lights people saw were just the flashlights of the people guarding the poppies through the night. And there were plenty of people sampling the goods, if you know what I mean, so hallucinations were not that uncommon. There was a heavy spirit of some kind in that house. I don't know any better way to describe it but that. It was like this oppressive kind of sadness. Maybe it was just a family falling apart. I don't know. But haunted?" She shrugged. "I don't know about that."

"Are you in touch with any of the family today?" Meredith asked.

"There honestly aren't that many of them left," Ruby said. "Willie passed when Lyle was little, and his mom and dad were gone by then too. And Laurel died before I met Willie. I don't really know much about the other siblings, to be honest. The only one who really keeps in touch is Sadie."

"Wait. You're in touch with Sadie?" Meredith couldn't believe it.

"She was always kind," Ruby said. "She always sent gifts on Lyle's birthday, and she sent a gift when I married Mitch. She sends cards at Christmas."

"So you know how to get in touch with her?"

"Oh yes. She lives not too far from here, right by Washington Square. I have her address and phone number, if you want it."

Meredith looked over at Julia, who nodded. She didn't need to say it. Finally, it looked like they were about to get the answers they'd been searching for all along.

Chapter Sixteen

SADIE DIDN'T ANSWER THE PHONE when Meredith called as soon as they were out of the clock shop, so Meredith left a message.

"She'll call us back. I can feel it," Julia said.

Meredith wasn't so sure. So far, the people who had been the closest to the Buford family had been the least likely to want to talk about them. "Let's go by her house and see if she's there."

"I don't see what harm it could do to pop in," Julia said with a smile.

They found Sadie's home easily. It was a beautiful brick Italianate home, with fluted entry columns and a gently sloping roof, right across from Washington Park.

"Sadie has come a long way from Ebenezer Creek," Julia said giving a low whistle.

They walked up the flagstone path and rang the doorbell.

A man answered the door. He was tall and had thick gray hair and a tan, and he had a healthy, outdoorsy look that reminded Meredith of Beau.

"Hello," he said, in the soft drawl that pegged him a Savannah native. "How can I help you?"

"Hi there. I'm Meredith Bellefontaine, and this is Julia Foley." Meredith held out her hand. She heard soft classical music playing inside the house. "We are doing research into the old Buford home out in Ebenezer Creek, and we were hoping to talk to Sadie."

The man's face changed at the mention of Ebenezer Creek; his smile faded, and his eyes became stormy. "Who did you say you were with?"

"We're private investigators, working for the party that bought the property." Meredith did her best to appear unassuming. You never could tell how people were going to respond to the news that she and Julia were PIs.

"Ruby Stone gave us her contact information," Julia added, no doubt hoping that would assuage his obvious concerns.

"I'm afraid Sadie isn't available at the moment," he said. Meredith saw a Queen Anne-style sideboard just inside the door.

"Can you tell us a time when she might be available to speak to us?" Meredith asked.

"I'm afraid I couldn't say," he said.

"Would you be able to tell us anything about the Buford home and family?" Meredith knew she was stretching.

"I'm afraid I could not." Apparently, he knew it too.

Would not, more like, but the effect was the same.

Julia, undeterred, was already holding out a business card. "If she does become available, could you please ask her to call this number?"

The man looked down at the card, pursed his lips, and nodded.

"I'll pass it along," he said. He moved his hand to the door, about to close it, but then he stopped. "Did you say someone finally bought that old place?"

"The sale closed last week. They're planning to knock down the house next week." Meredith hoped the news would instill some urgency, but she couldn't tell how it landed.

"I'll pass this along," he said, and they thanked him as he closed the door.

"What do you think the chances are she actually calls?" Julia asked.

"Slim to none."

Meredith thought their odds were about the same. They were so close and yet so far.

***

Meredith arrived at Monterey Square a good half an hour before she expected Aaron to pass through. She knew that he passed by this way just about every day on his way home from Jimmy's, and today she was ready. She'd gathered her gardening gloves, a shovel and trowel, several pots of mums, and, most importantly, several jumbo-sized bags of potting soil.

No one gave her a second look as she left the soil on the ground and arranged her gardening supplies inside the waist-high iron fence that surrounded the monument to Casimir Pulaski, an army general who died during the Battle of Savannah in the Mexican-American War. Many of the gardens in town were maintained by a crew of older women who weeded and planted and pruned in their spare time. Anyone passing by would have assumed she was just one of them. But as Meredith knelt down on the soil, she wasn't looking at the flower beds that ran inside the fence but at the stone path that led toward Taylor Street. No one seemed to notice. That was the beauty of being a middle-aged woman. You were mostly invisible. No one ever expected a PI to look like she did, and there were times when it *worked* to her advantage. Hopefully, like this one. Aaron should be coming down the path soon....

Meredith did her best to act natural, pinching off dead blooms and trying for all the world to look like she knew what she was doing. But she kept glancing up every thirty seconds or so, trying to make sure she didn't miss him.

And then, finally, there he was, strolling down the path like he didn't have a care in the world. He wore cargo shorts and a T-shirt with sneakers and his familiar Braves cap. Meredith set her phone to record, placed it mostly out of sight on the fence, and waited until he was almost across from her, and then she called out, "Excuse me!"

He didn't turn, and she realized he had earbuds in. She tried again, louder this time. "Hi there! Excuse me!"

This time he turned, and, taking one earbud out, smiled and turned toward her.

"Hello." He had a friendly smile. He glanced toward the trowel in her gloved hands and the heavy bags of soil on the far side of the iron fence and asked, "Do you need some help, ma'am?"

In that moment, she had a jolt of doubt. He was such a nice guy. Surely he couldn't really be cheating his employer, could he? But she knew there were plenty of nice guys with good Southern manners that lied, stole, and cheated. She needed to find out for sure about Aaron.

"That would be wonderful. These bags of soil are so heavy." She smiled helplessly. Truly, they *were* heavy—she'd made sure she got the heaviest ones she could—though she could lift them if she wanted to.

"It's no problem." Without hesitation, he bent over, picked up the first bag of soil, and hoisted it over the fence. He leaned over the fence as far as he could before he let it drop to the ground inside. Then he bent back over, picked up the second, and moved it inside the fence without any problem.

Not bad for a guy with a debilitating back injury, she thought.

"Thank you so much." Meredith gave him her best grateful smile, and he nodded, told her again that it was no problem, and then slipped his earbud back into his ear and moved along.

And with that, Meredith had the evidence she needed to nail Aaron Whitaker.

Chapter Seventeen

AFTER CHURCH ON SUNDAY, MEREDITH declined brunch with her friends and went instead to the farmer's market, where she bought a beautiful bouquet of lilies and roses and ranunculus. Ron had brought her stargazer lilies when he'd picked her up for their first date, and she'd always associated the fragrant flowers with him. Then she drove to the cemetery that sat up on a hill overlooking the river. She made her way to the Bellefontaine plot, with a stone statue of an angel and headstones for several generations of the family. Meredith had always found graveyards to be beautiful and peaceful. She liked to think about the generations that came before, and the ones that would come behind, and the fate that awaited all of them.

Today, as she set the flowers down in front of Ron's headstone, she cried a little less than she had last time, and that time she'd cried a little less than the time before. It was hard to come out here and see his name engraved in that tombstone, to see the date of his death, just two years and a week in the past, and know that the empty space in the ground next to him would hold her empty shell at some point too. But she also knew that she would see him again someday, and this separation was only temporary.

She stood in front of his headstone, remembering their wedding day, how he'd nearly passed out at the altar and how sweetly he'd kissed her once the minister had pronounced them married. She thought about how her mother had cried, and how happy she had been that she was finally married to the man of her dreams.

She remembered seeing Ron holding a newborn Carter, and how afraid he'd been that he'd break him, and how he'd held her when they'd lost the baby between Carter and Chase. She thought about how he'd coached Chase's Little League team, and taken the boys to the driving range so many times, and how proud he'd been standing up at Carter's wedding, toasting the newly married couple. Ron had loved his work, and he'd loved his family, and he'd loved history and his collections and trains.

And he'd also loved to come here and watch the boats, she thought, turning around to take in the view of the river from this perch. Fishing vessels, probably much like the one Willie Buford had worked on, sailed up and down the waters, heading toward the port. Pleasure boats with colorful sails and powerful motors moved past, as well as several larger cabin-style cruisers. A paddle-wheeled riverboat chugged downstream, showing off the city's rich heritage to tourists and visitors. There was always so much going on along the river, so much life happening just beyond these quiet, somber hills.

Meredith took in a deep breath and let it out slowly. She wasn't really ready to say goodbye to Ron. She probably never would be. But there was no reason she had to rush her grief, she knew. She could take her time and keep his things in the guest room a little longer. She could hold on to her memories and let life keep moving forward.

Just as she was about to turn to head home, her cell phone rang, breaking the stillness. She dug her phone out of her purse and looked down at the screen. She didn't recognize the number, but it was local. She hesitated. She would normally let a call like this go straight to voice mail, but she decided to pick this one up.

"Hello?"

"Oh. Hello. Is this Meredith Bellefontaine?" It was a woman, and she sounded uncertain.

"Yes, this is Meredith."

"Hello there, I'm...well, I'm not really sure what you're after, but my husband told me you came by yesterday, hoping to talk to me about the old house."

It was Sadie. Meredith tried to keep the excitement she felt out of her voice and remain calm and poised as she answered, "Yes, thank you so much for calling me back. My partner and I are working with a client to find out about the history of the home, and I was hoping you might be willing to talk to me about it."

"Henry said the old place has finally been sold?"

"That's right."

"I suppose it will be torn down?"

"I think it would be difficult to save it, given the state of the place," she answered carefully.

"I suppose it's probably fallen into ruin by now," Sadie said. Was that sadness in her voice? Or was it something else?

"Is there any chance you'd be willing to meet with me and my partner to talk about the house, and what happened?" Meredith hoped she hadn't pushed too far. She couldn't exactly come out and ask Sadie over the phone to tell her what happened to drive her family out. Ideally, an in-person conversation would make this all a lot more natural.

"What happened?" Sadie repeated.

"To the house," Meredith said smoothly. "Why it was left in the state it was."

Sadie didn't answer for a moment, and Meredith feared she was about to hang up. But then she said, "I don't really know what you mean."

Meredith tried to make sense of this, to understand what Sadie was getting at. It almost sounded like…like she didn't realize what it had looked like inside.

"When was the last time you were in the house?" Meredith asked.

"Oh goodness. Not since Daddy, probably. I wasn't…" Her voice broke off. "There wasn't a lot of reason to go back after that, and my brothers…" Again, she trailed off, and this time she was quiet for long enough that Meredith began to wonder if she had hung up. But she let the silence stretch out, and finally, Sadie continued. "We didn't really see eye to eye, you see. And it got ugly, and so…"

Meredith didn't see but she wanted to.

"My therapist has been urging me to go back out there and face it," Sadie finally said. "And I suppose, if I'm honest, I'd like to see the old place one more time before it's gone for good."

Meredith tried to keep her voice neutral so she didn't scare Sadie away with her excitement. "I would be happy to meet you out there. When would be a good time for you to go?"

This time, Sadie didn't hesitate. "I'll meet you there at five."

"Today?" Meredith couldn't believe it.

"I'll be there."

***

Meredith immediately called Julia, who was in the middle of preparing a standing rib roast. She abandoned the rib roast to get ready for the drive out to Ebenezer Creek. Meredith also called Rachel, who was free and agreed to meet them all out at the property to see the woman who had grown up there.

Meredith and Julia were the first to arrive, and as they walked up onto the porch, Meredith heard a door slam somewhere inside the house.

"What was that?"

Julia's eyes were wide, and she shook her head.

"Someone is inside," Meredith said, and then she rushed in and ran into the dining room, the living room, the kitchen. Julia rushed up the stairs, but she came back down a moment later shaking her head.

"We both heard a door slam, right?" Julia asked.

"And the back door is still boarded shut."

"That's right." Julia glanced toward the back of the house, where they could see the door still boarded over.

"Could it have been in the basement?" Meredith asked.

"I mean, I guess so. It was loud enough that I would have thought it was up here, but I guess the basement is where we know someone was before. But the only way out of the basement is up those stairs"— she pointed at the stairs that led to the cellar—"and no one came out of them."

Meredith looked around the decaying entryway, with the musty stairs that rose toward the second floor, the peeling wallpaper, and the warped floorboards. She wasn't making this up.

"Someone else was in this house," Meredith said. "And they just left, somehow."

"It's the only logical explanation," Julia agreed. "Because there is no such thing as ghosts."

Meredith didn't know what to say. She knew Julia had to be right, and yet she didn't see how.

Just then, they heard the sound of a car kicking up the gravel of the drive.

"Someone's here," Meredith said. Julia nodded and led her back out the front door and to the porch. Rachel's car was coming up the long curved lane. They waved, and Rachel stepped out and met them on the porch.

"Do you guys smell smoke?"

Meredith sniffed, and she smelled it too.

"It's probably neighbors burning leaves again," Julia said.

"It's a bit early in the season for that, isn't it?" Rachel asked.

Julia shrugged. "It's been like this the past few times we've been out here. Maybe the old place just smells like smoke."

Meredith wasn't sure any of them bought that, but no one offered another explanation. Meredith chose not to mention the fire remnants in the basement. They'd have to recheck that before they left.

"So. Have you found out if we have a ghost on our hands?" Rachel asked with a smile.

"There is no ghost. I'm sure of that," Meredith said. "But I'm hoping Sadie can tell us why people think there is," Meredith said. She checked her watch. It was already a few minutes past five. What if Sadie had changed her mind? Would she come after all?

They all stood there on the porch, waiting in the looming quiet. The minute hand on her watch kept moving. And then, just as Meredith was beginning to accept that they'd been stood up, she heard a car engine.

A luxury SUV finally came into view, driving slowly on the rutted dirt drive, and Meredith strained to catch a glimpse of the only member of the Buford family they'd managed to track down. The car rounded the bend, and the driver parked it behind their own cars, and then the car doors opened and Sadie stepped out of the driver's side. Her red hair had faded into a soft yellowish white, and she wore heavy-framed eyeglasses, and she was shorter than Meredith had expected, but it was unmistakably her. The man they'd met the day before climbed out of the passenger side and looked up at the house, his eyes wide.

"Sadie," Meredith said, rushing forward down the steps to meet her. "I'm Meredith Bellefontaine. Thank you so much for meeting us here."

Sadie gave her a sad smile and a nod and reached out to shake Julia's and Rachel's hands. Then she introduced her husband, Henry, but her eyes kept being drawn, inexorably, toward the house.

"Wow," Henry said. "You told me it was big, but I had no idea."

Meredith realized that this was the first time Henry was seeing the place where his wife grew up.

Meredith looked back at the caved-in roof, the falling shingles, the vines growing out of the windows. And she saw the proud columns resting on their pilasters, and the dozen glass windows framed by wooden shutters, and the twin fireplaces at each end of the house.

For just a moment, she saw that house as it must have once been, and she understood the gravity of what had been lost.

"It's worse than I imagined," Sadie finally said. There was sadness in her voice, mixed with something else Meredith couldn't ascertain. "They just left it here to rot."

Meredith had so many questions, but she knew she had to be patient. She needed to let Sadie process this before she started asking for answers.

"Would you like to see the inside?" Meredith asked, and then felt silly. She didn't need to invite Sadie in. This had been her home.

"I don't know," Sadie finally answered. Meredith appreciated her honesty.

"You've come all this way," Henry said softly, taking his wife's hand.

She nodded but didn't move forward.

"This house doesn't hold a lot of good memories," Sadie finally said. Meredith understood it as an explanation for why she was hesitating. "My family... Well, I suppose all families are complicated."

Meredith and Julia waited, and then they followed silently behind Sadie as she walked past them and inside the front door. There were tears in her eyes as she took in the decaying stairs, the peeling wallpaper, and the rotting wood. Meredith caught the scent of burning leaves again, stronger this time, but there was no smoke that she could see.

No one said anything as Sadie led them through the dining room, the kitchen, and the parlor. Sadie headed up the stairs and into each of the bedrooms. She stepped into the room with the purple bedspread and gently stroked the dress draped over the chair. Meredith guessed that this might have been hers. And then, without a word, she led them back out the front door again. They stood in the yard as the sun slipped below the tree line.

"I had no idea," she finally said. "I had no idea nothing was kept up." She brushed away a tear with the back of her hand. The smell of smoke still hung in the air, and it was stronger now, but Meredith couldn't place which direction it was coming from.

"When was the last time you were in the house?" Julia asked softly.

"1986," Sadie said. "When we buried Daddy."

"Buried him?" Meredith hadn't seen a headstone for Earl in the cemetery.

"He's buried next to Mama. We were going to get a headstone, but we never could agree on who would pay for it or what it should be like, so…" She shrugged helplessly.

Meredith tried to wrap her mind around this. The family had just never ordered a headstone for their father? That just wasn't done, not around these parts anyway.

"That's kind of the theme of this whole chapter of her life," Henry said. "Entropy by way of dissent."

Rachel cocked her head, and Meredith tried to parse the sentence in her head, but Julia jumped in. "You mean all of this…" She swept her hand around but didn't seem to be able to find the words to say what she was trying to get at.

"What happened here?" Meredith finally asked. "We started off assuming that something dramatic had happened to chase your family away overnight. Sickness or a direct threat or something like that. Something dramatic that would make them all up and leave in the middle of whatever they were doing—eating breakfast, putting a dress away, that sort of thing. But the more we learned, the more we wondered if it was something else."

"I almost wish it had been something as dramatic as all that," Sadie said. "It would be a better explanation than what really happened. Far less shameful."

Meredith waited for Sadie to go on.

"We never intended for the county to take the house," Sadie said with a deep breath. "This land had belonged to our grandparents and their grandparents before them. Around these parts, that means something."

Meredith nodded. She didn't know if a family's connection to their land was as strong and meaningful in other parts of the country, but she knew that in the South, the place where you came from was inextricably linked to who you were.

"But after Mama passed, well, things just kind of fell apart. Eldan dropped out and joined the army, and Willie was off working on the fishing boat. He and Daddy were like oil and water, and he was smart enough to get out before their fights turned into something worse. Nellie married the first chance she got, and poor Laurel... Well, Mama never got over that. How could you? So it was just me and Jed left in the house when Daddy was killed. None of us ever thought about things like wills, but you expect them to be there when you need them. And there wasn't one. I guess Daddy never got around to making one."

"It can be hard for people to think about their own deaths," Julia said quietly.

Sadie nodded. "I do get that, even more as I get older. But it sure is a pain for those left behind when there isn't clear direction for what is to be done with things like the family home."

"Especially when you have a group of five siblings that couldn't agree on what to have for dinner, let alone how to handle an estate," Henry added.

"Jed was still in high school. We can't hold him responsible," Sadie said. "Eldan and Nellie wanted no part of it and wanted to sell it. But Nellie thought the money should be divided five ways, while Willie thought that as the oldest, it should all go to him, like it had to the oldest male in every generation before him."

"But others didn't want to sell it?" Meredith asked gently.

"Jed needed a place to live, and I couldn't see letting go of the ancestral land. I didn't think it was ours to sell, even though I didn't want to live here myself. Willie didn't seem to care one way or the other, as long as he got his cut."

"You didn't want to sell the land, but you didn't want to live here yourself?" Julia asked, her head cocked.

"This place..." She let out a sigh. "I don't have a lot of happy memories of this place, especially once Mama passed."

"It was a difficult childhood," Henry added. He placed his hand on the small of his wife's back. "Their father was...a hard man."

"For starters, he was a drug dealer," Sadie said with a wry laugh. "We didn't think about it like that at the time, of course. We knew what the poppies were for, but naturally we didn't think about what happened to the resin after it left our barn. It was just what our dad did, when we were kids. But when he drank too much, he got angry, and we learned early to run for cover," Sadie said. "He took it out on Willie, mostly, but the rest of us too sometimes. And it got worse the further into debt he went."

"So there was debt," Meredith said quietly.

"Oh goodness, yes. We didn't realize just how much until after he died, but we knew he was spending more time making runs to Savannah and was still behind, and the power would go off for stretches at a time, and there wasn't enough food. That kind of thing. And it was worse when he was sampling the goods, because then he worked less."

"You can understand why so many of the kids were eager to leave home." Henry rubbed his hand up and down his wife's back. "And why they had different ideas about how to handle the property."

"So what happened?" Meredith asked. "How did it end up like this?"

"We couldn't agree on what to do with it," Sadie said. "And in the meantime, no one was paying the taxes. Eldan and Nellie had the means but wouldn't pay until the fate of the property was decided. Willie didn't really have much to spare, and I don't think he would have kicked in anything even if he could have. And Jed and I…" She shrugged. "He was just a teenager, and I was working down at the library. For a while Jed tried to carry on Dad's business, but he couldn't do it on his own. I wanted no part of it. We were looking at a bill for thousands of dollars, and I couldn't cover it."

"So the bill just went unpaid?" Julia asked.

Sadie nodded. "And then the county seized the property. Came in one day and changed the locks on the doors, and that was that. Everything was left as it was, for all this time. I had already moved to town and had started attending college classes, and Jed moved in with our Uncle Hiram, and that was it. Willie died a few years later, and Eldan just a few years ago. I still see Jed sometimes. He lives in California now, and he has a family. But Nellie has nothing to do with the rest of us. Hasn't for decades."

It broke Meredith's heart to hear about this family, torn apart by greed and deception and pain. Sadie's story did explain how the house had come to be abandoned, but there was still one thing that didn't add up to Meredith.

"I guess I understand now why it looks like people were interrupted in the middle of a meal, or putting things away, if that's when the county came to change the locks," Meredith said. "But what I don't understand is, why didn't you and your brothers and sister take anything from the house? Why didn't you take your family's treasures when you left?"

"Treasures?" Sadie's confusion was plain on her face. "There aren't any treasures in that house."

"Like your mother's Bible, or your father's wallet or clothes. Photographs?"

Sadie shrugged. "What would we do with all of that stuff? It's all just junk. Relics from a time none of us particularly want to think too much about."

Meredith's heart broke just a little bit more to hear a family's memories dismissed just like that. But finally, at last, she understood. They hadn't fled the house with no time to grab their most precious possessions. It was that these possessions weren't precious; that the family believed their past was better off forgotten. Meredith held that thought for a moment, grieving over the tragedy of it all.

"What about ghosts?" Rachel asked quietly. "Is the house really haunted?"

"Only by bad memories," Sadie said, shaking her head. "I know people said all kinds of things. The place is drafty, so sometimes doors would close unexpectedly. And yeah, the floorboards would expand sometimes when the light hit them right, and that could make it sound like footsteps, so I guess I get it, kind of. But no, the only ghosts that haunt this place are broken dreams and bad feelings."

They all stayed quiet a minute, letting that sit. Could the sound of footsteps they'd heard really have been nothing more than wood expanding? Could doors slam because of the breeze inside the house? Or had there really been someone there? Meredith supposed either was possible.

"Do you smell smoke?" Henry finally asked.

Meredith didn't have to sniff this time. She nodded. The smell had increased, and she was pretty sure she wasn't imagining that she was smelling it more regularly now.

"We've smelled it every time we've been out here," Julia said. "And when we were here before, we found ashes in the basement. But that couldn't..." She let her voice trail off, watching as Sadie stepped off the porch and was walking into the yard now, sniffing. Meredith watched as she walked across the overgrown front yard and toward the corner of the house, and then disappeared.

Meredith and Julia looked at each other, and then they followed her. She was walking quickly across the side yard, where smaller trees, newly grown as nature reclaimed the land, joined the larger timbers that had stood for generations. She hurried through the woods toward the water, close to the decaying dock. Meredith froze when she saw smoke coming up from the ground.

"What in the world?"

"It's in the tunnel," Sadie said.

"The what?" Julia ran to catch up with her. Meredith followed a step behind, and saw flames licking at the wood of an old trap door built into the ground just before the dock. She knew there were tunnels that ran under parts of old Savannah. You could take tours of them, some said to date back to the days of pirates, and she'd seen tunnels that weren't accessible to the public and only rumored to exist. But it had never occurred to her that there would be underground tunnels out this way.

"The tunnel. For getting things to the boat unseen," Sadie said, staring uncomprehendingly at the smoke now billowing up out from the ground. "This was so Daddy could load and unload his… cargo without being seen leaving the house."

She turned and ran toward the creek, Henry just a few steps behind. Rachel had already pulled out her cell phone and was dialing 911 to report the fire. Meredith wasn't sure what to do, so she followed after Sadie and Henry, but at the water's edge, she saw there was nothing to haul water with.

"The tunnel leads to…" Meredith's voice dropped off.

"The basement," Sadie said.

"But we thought that when the basement stairs were blocked off, the only way into the basement was the cellar door, which was nailed shut," Meredith said.

"There's the door to the coal chute behind the old stove," Sadie said. "It hadn't been used for coal in generations when we were kids, and Granddaddy had it changed to go out to the dock."

Wait. What? "We didn't see anything like that," Meredith said.

"You wouldn't, unless you knew to look for it. It was well hidden."

So that had to be how someone had been getting into the basement, even with the interior door blocked off. Someone who had lit at least one fire in the basement.

"Someone must have used the tunnel to get into the basement again after the county blocked off the interior door," Julia surmised. "Maybe he lit a fire again, and when we came, we scared him off."

"That slamming door we heard," Meredith said, understanding dawning. "That might have been him escaping through the tunnel so he wouldn't be caught."

"Which means that most likely, the fire didn't start in the tunnel," Julia said, her eyes wide.

And somehow, the fire had gotten out of control when he left.

"I've got a gardening bucket in my car," Meredith suggested.

But Sadie was shaking her head. "I don't think a bucket is going to help at this point." She was looking toward the house, so Meredith also turned and saw smoke pouring out of the broken windows of the basement.

"Is that fire truck on its way?" Meredith called to Rachel, who nodded, the phone to her ear. But Meredith knew it would never get here in time. They were too far out, and it would have a hard time on that bumpy dirt road, and even now, the house, packed to the gills with dry, rotted wood, was starting to smoke.

"Let's all move away," Henry said, and she didn't know what else to do, so she followed him across the lawn. Clearly he had already come to terms with what she was still struggling to accept—that the Buford house was going up in flames.

Meredith wanted to do something to stop it, but she didn't know what could be done.

"What about the person who was in the tunnel? The one who made the fires?" Sadie asked.

"He's long gone, whoever he is," Meredith said. "The basement has been blocked off from the inside, so I think when he heard us come in, he scrambled, I guess out the tunnel door. He must not have put his fire out all the way in his haste to get out."

Sadie nodded. They stood in the yard and watched as flames traveled up the dining room curtains and windows on the second floor began to shatter from the heat. Smoke billowed out of the jagged gaps left behind.

Meredith glanced over at Rachel, who still had the phone to her ear, but was watching, her eyes wide. Julia was shaking her head, just a little, her mouth open. Henry had his arm around Sadie's waist, and Sadie had tears streaming down her face. Meredith couldn't even begin to imagine what was going through her mind as she watched her childhood home, the source of so much pain, being destroyed one lick of flame at a time.

Meredith didn't know a lot about fires, but she was surprised by how quickly it spread. They had just been inside that house a short time ago. She said a prayer of thanks that they had not been there when the fire spread to the main part of the house. This was bad, but it could have been so much worse. The darkening sky made the flames seem even brighter as they overtook the second story.

The house was going to be knocked down anyway, Meredith reminded herself. This wasn't a tragedy. The tragedy was that no one had cared enough about this house to try to save it years ago. The tragedy was a family torn apart, divided against itself.

Finally, she heard the sirens, off in the distance. Rachel was still talking to the dispatcher, giving directions to the dirt road, but the house continued to burn, and all they could do was watch. When the fire trucks finally pulled up in front of the house, the flames were shooting out of the roof. Meredith watched as the firefighters unfurled their hoses, but they didn't even attempt to aim their hoses at the house itself. Instead, they sprayed water on the trees surrounding the house, trying to keep the fire from spreading.

She didn't know how long they all stood there, watching the house burn and collapse in on itself, but eventually, when the sky was fully dark, the house had turned to nothing more than a pile of glowing rubble, and they finally turned to go. The fire department would be here for some time, making sure the fire was totally out, and Meredith was pretty sure she and the others would all need to talk to the police about what had happened, to tell what they had guessed about how the fire had started, and make sure they were not blamed for the fire. But for now, they finally had answers about what had happened in the house at Ebenezer Creek, and it was time to go home.

Chapter Eighteen

THE AIR HAD A CHILLY bite in it when the earth movers, brought in on the newly paved road, broke ground for the new boutique hotel. Meredith and Julia had wanted to be there to see the work begin, and though it was a bit eerie to see the plain flat ground where the house had once stood, it also felt clean, satisfying. A new beginning.

They'd learned that the fire had indeed been started by someone living in the house without permission. This explained the flashes of light and the noises Meredith had heard in the house when no one was supposed to be there. At one point, she'd guessed they had a long-lost family member possibly camping here without permission. But, now that everyone was accounted for, she knew it couldn't be.

Rachel, wearing a hard hat, stood nearby, and Meredith was glad to see her dream finally come true. This was such a gorgeous piece of land, in such a beautiful part of the world. She was glad to see it come back to life. Soon, visitors would come to see this majestic forest and to glide down the waters of the creek. It would be beautiful once again.

They watched for a while, and then Meredith and Julia took a walk to a spot just a ways downriver. They walked until they saw the signpost and then went right up to it until they could read it.

March to the Sea: Ebenezer Creek

One mile north, on December 9, 1864, during the American Civil War, US Gen. Jeff. C. Davis crossed Ebenezer Creek with his 14th Army Corps as it advanced toward Savannah during Gen. William T. Sherman's March to the Sea. Davis hastily removed the pontoon bridges over the creek, and hundreds of freed slaves following his army drowned trying to swim the swollen waters to escape the pursuing Confederates. Following a public outcry, Sec. of War Edwin Stanton met with Sherman and local black leaders in Savannah on January 12, 1865. Four days later, President Lincoln approved Sherman's Special Field Orders No. 15, confiscating over 400,000 acres of coastal property and redistributing it to former slaves in 40-acre tracts. -2010

"Maggie Lu's hard work finally paid off," Meredith said.

"It took far too long for this sign to be raised," Julia said, shaking her head. "But it finally happened."

Meredith wished she could go back and undo the injustices of history, but since she couldn't, the least they could do was mark them, to make sure people knew when a wrong had been done so they could do better in the future.

And here, almost a century and a half later, the hard work of several people, including Maggie Lu, had finally marked the spot where the Union army had turned on hundreds of African American men, women, and children.

It was a tragedy, a scar on the nation's history, but one that now would never be forgotten. Just as ruins of grandeur could give way to new beginnings and the scorched earth could fertilize the ground for new growth, there were always small glimmers of hope to be found in the worst tragedies if you looked for them.

Standing here, Meredith knew, more than ever before, that holding on to the past was important, and that even as memories faded, it was important not to let go of them. But she also knew that time moved forward, and as it went on, it dulled the sharp pain of loss and grief and despair and allowed for glimpses of possibility to come.

She had never been so sure of anything.

Dear Reader,

The idea for this mystery came from a radio story I heard about an abandoned house where the family left everything behind (it's *This American Life*, episode #199, called "The House on Loon Lake," if you want to check it out). Something about the image of a house, abandoned and left to rot with the family's treasures inside, wouldn't leave my mind, especially once I realized that the house in my story would be in the South, where kudzu and humid summers could add an extra layer of creepiness to the place as our sleuths tried to determine what happened to the family. I've clearly taken liberties, but I hope I've created a compelling setting for this story.

When I was trying to figure out where to set the house—I wanted it to be outside Savannah, but not too far outside—I stumbled upon pictures of Ebenezer Creek, and I knew that had to be it. The dramatic landscape looks like something from another planet, or at least another time, and I had never seen anything like it. I hope you enjoy learning about it as much as I did.

I had so much fun writing this book, and I hope you have fun reading it. Enjoy!

Signed,
Beth Adams

About the Author

BETH ADAMS LIVES IN BROOKLYN, New York, with her husband and two young daughters. When she's not writing, she spends her time cleaning up after two devious cats and trying to find time to read mysteries.

The Truth Behind the Fiction

I HAD NEVER HEARD OF the Tragedy at Ebenezer Creek until I started working on this book, and once I came across it, I wondered why I had never learned about it. The incident unfolds pretty much as Meredith explains in this story: Jefferson C. Davis (who is not the Confederate president, but a Union officer with a confusingly similar name) was leading his troops toward Savannah as part of Sherman's March to the Sea, and hundreds of freed slaves had begun to follow the troops, believing they were being led to freedom. But the growing group began to slow the army's progress and use more of its limited resources, and the Confederate soldiers were closing in on them.

When the army came to the banks of the swampy creek, they built a pontoon bridge and insisted that the troops cross first, and then Davis ordered the bridge destroyed, trapping the freed slaves on the the far side with the Confederates approaching. Hundreds were drowned or trampled trying to cross the creek to escape the Southern army, and the rest were mostly rounded up and returned to slavery. Though it is a shameful part of our history—or, more probably, because of it—a historical marker for the event was not erected until 2010.

MEREDITH'S SIMPLE GREEN BEANS

1 pound fresh green beans, ends snipped

3 tablespoons butter

4 cloves of garlic, chopped fine

zest of one lemon

salt and pepper to taste

Place green beans in a large pan and cover with water. Over medium-high heat, bring water to boil and simmer until the beans are starting to become tender, about five minutes. Drain and return to pan, along with butter, and cook two to three minutes more. Add garlic and cook until fragrant, another minute or so. Take off heat and top with lemon zest and plenty of salt and pepper.

*Read on for a sneak peek of another exciting book
in the Savannah Secrets series!*

The Weight of Years
By DeAnna Julie Dodson

"WE'RE PRETTY FULL THIS AFTERNOON," Julia Foley said, surveying the graceful elegance of the Savannah Historical Society's meeting room. With its lush draperies and tall white columns, intricately carved crown molding and gleaming parquet floor, it made her feel as if she were in the ballroom of a grand estate house before the Civil War. Her reflection in one of the pier glass mirrors made her almost wish that she had her silver hair swept up into a chignon and was wearing a dove-colored gown that would make her gray eyes sparkle—instead of her practical pink knit top, linen jacket, and black slacks.

Her friend and business partner, Meredith Bellefontaine, looked the room over too and nodded her curly blond head. "It's not every month the society gets to hear Miss Charlotte Lockwood speak."

"It's not every month anybody gets to hear Miss Charlotte Lockwood speak. Beatrice really outdid herself getting her to come."

"She did. And she won't hesitate to tell us about it either."

"Anyway, I don't blame Miss Charlotte for not getting out much anymore. If I were nearly ninety, I wouldn't do anything but exactly what I felt like doing."

"We've got another twenty-five years before we have to worry about that," Meredith said. "Who knows what we'll be up to by then?"

Julia started to answer and then turned her attention to the podium as Beatrice Enterline, the head of the historical society, began to speak.

"Good afternoon, ladies and gentlemen," she said, her hazel eyes bright with triumph. "I am sure that all of you have heard about the Alice Delorme Lockwood Foundation for Children, a foundation that has done so much to bring hope and happiness to Savannah's children since 1905. This afternoon, I am delighted to present to you one of Savannah's most celebrated citizens, the owner of the historic Delorme Estate and director for the past seventy years of the Lockwood Foundation, Miss Charlotte Delorme Lockwood."

As the applause sounded, Beatrice stepped away from the podium, and Miss Charlotte stepped forward, leaning on an ebony walking stick and on the arm of a heavyset, middle-aged black woman. She was small and elegant, her back as straight as her cane, her carriage as regal as any queen. Despite her years, her face was nearly unlined and her skin was luminous over the fine bones of her face and the blue veins of her hands. Her hair was white as new cotton and lay in a coiled braid on top of her head. It looked all the whiter set off by the pure black of the simple, full-skirted dress she wore. A string of large, but not too large, pearls with matching earrings completed the picture. Gracious, exquisite, and unyielding.

She stood with a slight smile on her face, waiting for the applause to die down, and then she stepped closer to the microphone.

"Thank you very much," she said, her voice stronger than Julia would have expected, marked with the soft edges of a Southern accent and with only the slightest quaver of age in it. "And my thanks to Mrs. Enterline for her kind invitation to speak to you all today. If you have been in Savannah long, you have most likely heard of the Lockwood Foundation. We are quite proud of our accomplishments for over a century in finding homes for children who have none. We have a long history of making resources available for those who are looking into the possibility of adoption or who have already opened their homes and hearts to these precious little ones. When we help bring a child into a family, that is only the beginning of the foundation's work. From that first moment, the Lockwood Foundation is there to see that the newly blended family grows stronger with each passing year."

Julia looked over at Meredith. So far this sounded like the beginning of an appeal for donations.

"But, as generous as Savannah has been in supporting our work," Miss Charlotte continued, "I am reminded that I am here this afternoon to talk not about the present or the future but the past. My great-grandmother, Alice Delorme Lockwood, was born on the Delorme Estate in 1859." She smiled mischievously. "That was a very long time ago, even for me. She was raised in the war, as she liked to say, and lived all her life in a struggle of one kind or other. She outlived her family, her husband, her son, and her grandson, my father. My parents died when I was very young and my grandparents well before then, but Grandmama brought me up in the great tradition of the Delormes, teaching me what it meant to bear the name and the duties that came with it. I remember her in the days before she died. She was ninety years old then, a milestone I will soon reach, and still running the estate and the foundation to suit herself."

For the next twenty minutes, Miss Charlotte spoke of the things her great-grandmother had told her about Savannah of the 1860s and '70s, of the Civil War and of Reconstruction, of how society changed, sometimes painfully, over time, of innovations and set-backs, bitter conflicts and eventual understanding. Her voice grew stronger as she went on, and the light in her pale blue eyes seemed to intensify as she told Alice's story, much of it Savannah's story, to her rapt audience.

"Then," she said at last, "the summer I turned eighteen, she sat me down and told me she was placing the estate, the foundation, and the honor of the name into my hands. How she knew it was time, I don't know, but it was only six hours later that she went to sleep in the sun on the back veranda and never woke up." She glanced back at the black woman who was sitting behind her, who had watched her protectively, almost anxiously, the whole while she spoke. "My dear Brenda is here. It was her grandmother, Hannah, who found Grandmama and came to tell me she was gone. And when I went to her, she looked sweetly at rest, and I knew she had made her peace."

By then, Julia felt a pang of loss. It was not only for Alice Lockwood, but for all she had known and done in her long life. For all those things that people now could read about and have told to them but would never really know, not in the same way Alice had known them. Or the same way Miss Charlotte knew them now. Before long, even her memories would be buried under the weight of years.

"One day soon, I will also have to pass on the estate and the foundation," Miss Charlotte said in closing, "but they will both continue on in memory of, and in the tradition of, Alice Delorme Lockwood, for the love of Savannah and its children."

She stood there for a moment, nodding in gracious acknowledgment of the audience's applause, but she seemed to wilt a little, sinking into herself, the animation of her storytelling gone. Brenda came up beside her and took her arm, helping her to a chair as Beatrice came back to the podium.

"Thank you so much, Miss Charlotte, for that wonderful talk. Did y'all enjoy that?"

The applause swelled, and Miss Charlotte nodded her appreciation, looking too spent to do more.

"Would you like Miss Charlotte to come back?" Beatrice asked, and again there was applause.

"How amazing that must have been," Meredith whispered to Julia. "Actually talking to someone who lived through the Civil War and everything that came afterward."

"Miss Charlotte is quite a speaker," Julia whispered back as Beatrice thanked her guest, reminded everyone to give generously to the Lockwood Foundation, and then moved on to the business portion of the meeting. "She must really rake in the donations for her charity."

"I bet."

"I don't know if she'll remember me from the fundraiser she spoke at last year, but I'd love to say hello to her again."

"Do you know Miss Lockwood?" an unfamiliar voice asked.

Julia and Meredith both turned to the young woman sitting behind them.

"I really enjoyed her talk," she continued, a light in her golden-brown eyes. "Do you think they'd let me meet her? I wouldn't keep her long, but I'd love to say hello to her."

Julia smiled. "If she stays after the meeting," she said, keeping her voice low, "I'm going to say hello. Would you like to come with me?"

The woman's blond spiral curls bounced with the enthusiastic nodding of her head.

Fortunately for everyone, Beatrice kept the boring parts of the meeting short and to the point, and soon it was dismissed. Several people made a beeline toward Miss Charlotte.

"We'd better hurry if we're going to get a chance to talk to her," Julia said. "She already looks worn out."

"Thanks for letting me go with you," the young woman said, getting to her feet. She couldn't have been more than two or three inches over five feet tall. "My name's Jaden Browning."

Julia shook her hand. "I'm Julia Foley. This is my friend and business partner, Meredith Bellefontaine."

"Good to meet you," Meredith said, shaking Jaden's hand too. "Do you live in Savannah?"

They walked toward where Miss Charlotte was sitting. Beatrice was standing over her, chattering away, no doubt gushing over how lovely it was to have the head of the Lockwood Foundation speak at her own little old historical society.

"Dallas, actually," Jaden said. "I'm getting my degree in journalism at UTD."

"UTD?" Meredith asked.

"The University of Texas at Dallas. I still have a semester to go, but I heard about Miss Lockwood speaking here today, and I thought I'd take a chance and come hear her."

Julia raised her eyebrows. "That's a long way to come for a twenty-minute talk, isn't it?"

"Well, yes and no." Jaden's grin wrinkled the dusting of freckles on her nose. "I was assigned to do a paper on her foundation in one of my classes a little while back, and I've been interested in her ever since. She'd know better than anybody what Alice Lockwood was like and, not trying to be grim or anything, but she's nearly ninety. She's not going to be around forever. If anybody's going to write a real book about Alice Lockwood and the foundation, it's got to be done pretty soon."

"So you came not for the talk but for the introduction."

Jaden nodded. "But it was a wonderful talk, wasn't it? Maddening though. Just enough to whet my appetite. There's so much I'd like to know. I mean, she's actually spoken to somebody who lived back then."

The corners of Meredith's mouth turned up. Julia knew they both understood Jaden's excitement and her desire to salvage whatever was left of Alice Lockwood's tales and Miss Charlotte's memories of them.

They had to wait only a few more minutes for their turn to talk to Miss Charlotte, thanks to a minor crisis on the other side of the room that demanded Beatrice's attention. Beatrice excused herself, but by then Miss Charlotte looked exhausted. Still, she smiled serenely and welcomed Julia, Meredith, and Jaden to sit by her.

"Of course I remember you, Mrs. Foley. You helped raise a good deal of money for the foundation, and I am very grateful."

"I was happy to help. And, please, do call me Julia. This is my friend, Meredith Bellefontaine."

"Mrs. Bellefontaine," Miss Charlotte said with a nod. "I met your husband several years ago. Please accept my condolences on his passing."

Meredith looked surprised and touched. "Thank you. I didn't realize you knew him. I miss him very much, but my memories are happy."

Jaden looked at Julia expectantly.

"And this is Jaden Browning," Julia told Miss Charlotte. "We just met her, but she enjoyed your talk so much, she was hoping you wouldn't mind if we introduced her to you."

"I didn't like to barge up here and start talking," Jaden said.

"Very polite of you, Miss Browning." Miss Charlotte wasn't quite smiling, but she looked indulgent. "So many these days, young and old, never take thought for the niceties."

"No, ma'am," Jaden said. "I guess they don't much anymore. But I think it's only right to show respect."

Miss Charlotte seemed pleased with that.

"And did you enjoy our little talk, Miss Browning?" she asked just as her assistant came up beside her and touched her forearm lightly.

"We don't want to overdo, Miss Charlotte, I'm sure."

Miss Charlotte patted her hand fondly. "No, Brenda, I suppose we don't. I hope you ladies will excuse us."

Brenda helped her to her feet and gave her her cane.

"Oh," Jaden breathed.

Miss Charlotte turned back to her, one silvery eyebrow raised.

"Oh, no, I'm sorry, ma'am," Jaden said, her face turning a little pink. "I know you must be tired, but I had really hoped I could talk to you for a few minutes. After coming all this way, I mean."

"From where did you come?" Miss Charlotte asked.

"From Dallas. I'm in school there. Journalism. I was really hoping…" She trailed off under Brenda's disapproving stare. "I know you're tired. I'm so glad to have met you anyway. Thank you. I really enjoyed your talk."

"Thank you. It means a great deal to me to hear that. Was there something specific you wished to talk about, Miss Browning?"

Jaden glanced at Julia, and then turned again to Miss Charlotte. "I want to write a book."

The almost-breathless admission brought a twinkle to the older woman's eye.

"Do you now? What sort of a book?"

"About Alice Lockwood and her foundation. I mean I want to write about you both, since she raised you and you took over her work after she died." Jaden managed a tremulous smile. "You know so much about her, I was hoping you would let me write it all down before it's too late." She caught a quick breath and put one hand over her mouth. "I mean, uh, before I have to go back home and—"

"You mean while I'm still around to tell you about her."

That twinkle was still in Miss Charlotte's eye.

"Oh, ma'am—"

"No need to get all flustered. Truth is truth. I know how old I am, and I know I'm on the wrong end of a long life." Miss Charlotte put one finger under Jaden's chin and tilted up her face. "I think a book would be a fine idea. What I remember of Grandmama should not be lost once I'm gone. What do you expect to make from writing this sort of book? Or maybe it's the fame you're after."

Jaden's blush deepened. "Oh, no, ma'am. I know historical biographies usually aren't bestsellers. I don't mind that. But everything your great-grandmother told you firsthand about her life, I would hate for all that to be lost."

"So you're going to write it just because of that?"

Jaden nodded.

"And you don't expect any money from it?"

"Not in particular, no."

"And what if I said I would grant you whatever interviews you'd like, as they fit into my schedule, of course, on the condition that you would donate the proceeds to my foundation?"

Again Jaden nodded, this time with a touch of a smile on her face. "I'd like that."

Julia glanced over at Meredith, sure her partner was as surprised by the exchange as she was.

Miss Charlotte looked the young woman over coolly. "And you get nothing out of it but the satisfaction of having done it?"

"Well, there is one thing," Jaden admitted.

Again, Miss Charlotte raised one fine brow.

"I was hoping to use it for my master's thesis too. I mean if you wouldn't mind." Jaden's expression was touched with a sudden bit of mischief. "I'm not sure if I want to be a novelist or work for one of the big papers when I'm through with school, but having my name on a book cover sure wouldn't hurt either way."

Miss Charlotte laughed softly. "I think that would be the least you should get from it." She patted Jaden's shoulder. "Well, not to worry. If I were to guess, I'd say we could work out between us more equitable terms than that. Brenda, would you please give Miss Browning one of my cards? And if she will be kind enough to call sometime tomorrow afternoon, I'm sure you will be able to find a time that would be mutually convenient for both of us to have a pleasant talk about Grandmama."

"Yes, Miss Charlotte," Brenda said, "as soon as you sit back down here and rest yourself."

She helped the older lady get comfortable once more and then dug in her purse for a business card.

"If you'd call sometime tomorrow afternoon, Miss Browning," Brenda said, handing Jaden the card, "I'll be able to check Miss Charlotte's schedule for you."

"Oh, thank you," Jaden said, clutching the card against her heart.

"If either of you would like to join us, Mrs. Bellefontaine, Mrs. Foley," Miss Charlotte said, "you're both very welcome. I understand you both were born and raised here in Savannah. Maybe you can help me keep my facts in order when I have to answer the young lady's questions and not just rattle off what I memorized for my speech."

"Oh, we'd love to," Julia said. "We stay pretty busy of course, but we have room in our schedule, don't we?" She looked at Meredith questioningly.

"We can certainly check. I know I'd love to come."

"Before the meeting began, Meredith and I were saying how wonderful it would be to know more of what your great-grandmother's life was like."

"I know you have a lot more you could tell about her than you could in only the few minutes they gave you here at the meeting," Meredith added.

"We're agreed then," Miss Charlotte said, and she laid her hand on Brenda's sturdy arm. "Please give each of these ladies my card."

"Yes, Miss Charlotte."

"I'm thinking now that a nice luncheon at home would be agreeable to all of us," Miss Charlotte said as Brenda handed out two more of her cards. "Would all of you enjoy that?"

"Oh, yes, please," Jaden said, clasping her hands together.

"Very well then. If you will each give your telephone number to Brenda, we'll be able to settle things easily."

Brenda took down their numbers and put the slip of paper into the small planning journal she carried with her.

"Now," Miss Charlotte said, "I will discuss the matter with Brenda this afternoon, and she will call each of you tomorrow to see if the time we choose will serve. Good afternoon."

With her ebony cane and Brenda's assistance, Miss Charlotte stood and made her way out of the room.

"Wow," Jaden said, her hands still clasped together with the business card between them. "Oh, wow. It's almost like talking to Alice Lockwood herself."

"It is a little, isn't it?" Julia asked. "She does have that effect on people."

"Thank you so much," Jaden gushed. "I would never have gotten to talk to her, and I especially wouldn't have gotten invited to lunch at the Delorme Estate, if you hadn't introduced us."

"I didn't expect we'd be invited too," Meredith said. "I've visited the estate before, only the places that are open to the public, of course, and I've seen the grape arbors and the fields of vegetables and soybeans, but I never thought I'd actually be invited for lunch there."

"I didn't know Miss Charlotte knew Ron before he died," Julia said. "Or that she knew he died."

She looked at the card Brenda had given her. It was as elegant as the woman whose name it bore, black raised script on off-white linen cardstock with Miss Charlotte's contact information and, in the lower left corner, a faint etching of the Delorme Estate, Corinthian columns and all.

"Miss Charlotte may not get out much," Meredith said, "but it sounds to me like she keeps track of everything that happens in Savannah. I hadn't thought about it for years, but now I remember Ron did do some work for her. Background check on someone she wanted to hire, if I remember right."

"Oh, really? Hire to do what?"

Meredith frowned. "I can't remember now. There's probably some record in the office. We'll check it out."

"I want to thank you both again," Jaden said. "This is so exciting, I can hardly stand it. I've got to go find something to wear when we have lunch at the Delorme Estate."

With a soft little shriek, Jaden hurried away.

Meredith smiled and shook her head. "At least we've made somebody ecstatically happy today."

"She's cute, isn't she, with that curly hair and turned-up nose? I was kind of surprised, though, when she agreed to Miss Charlotte's terms about the book. She'll be doing all that work writing it and get nothing for it."

Meredith shrugged. "Well, if she can use it for her thesis as well as a start in the writing business, that might not be such a bad deal in the long run."

"Yeah," Julia replied. "That would be okay...if that's all she's after."

A Note from the Editors

WE HOPE YOU ENJOY THE Savannah Secrets series, created by the Books and Inspirational Media Division of Guideposts, a nonprofit organization that touches millions of lives every day through products and services that inspire, encourage, help you grow in your faith, and celebrate God's love in every aspect of your daily life.

Thank you for making a difference with your purchase of this book, which helps fund our many outreach programs to military personnel, prisons, hospitals, nursing homes, and educational institutions. To learn more, visit GuidepostsFoundation.org.

We also maintain many useful and uplifting online resources. Visit Guideposts.org to read true stories of hope and inspiration, access OurPrayer network, sign up for free newsletters, download free e-books, join our Facebook community, and follow our stimulating blogs.

To learn about other Guideposts publications, including the bestselling devotional *Daily Guideposts*, go to ShopGuideposts.org, call (800) 932-2145, or write to Guideposts, PO Box 5815, Harlan, Iowa 51593.

Sign up for the
Guideposts Fiction Newsletter

and stay up-to-date on the books you love!

guideposts fiction

Inspiring reads chosen just for you!

What's New

Ordinary Women of the Bible

This one-of-a-kind series that brings you page-turning stories enriched with biblical and historical facts, which allow you to see how God called on everyday women to work His will. These groundbreaking stories are a thrilling way to experience God's love and power. These stories will open your heart as you immerse yourself in their world and see how they lived and worked...the difficulties they struggled with almost daily... their customs and traditions...and the hopes and dreams they held dear. You'll see how their faith, devotion, and love for God carried them through unimaginable situations. Learn More

Reader Favorite

Secrets of Wayfarers Inn

Secrets of Wayfarers Inn is everything you love in a great mystery: intriguing plots, secrets from the past, and faith-filled characters with the added excitement of unexpected surprises from one of the most unique periods in American history. The historic town of Marietta, Ohio, once an important stop on the Underground Railroad, is the setting for these thrilling mysteries. You'll love piecing together clues from the past that help unravel present-day mysteries. And you'll absolutely adore the energetic trio of friends who have vowed to never let their lives be boring. Learn More

From Our Editors

Mysteries of Lancaster County

Welcome to Bird-in-Hand, Pennsylvania, a quaint village in the heart of Lancaster County's Amish Country. It's here, amid rolling green hills and well-tended farms, where the Classen sisters, Elizabeth, Martha, and Mary, reunite after inheriting their family home. Together, they operate Secondhand Blessings, a charming gift-and-thrift store, housed in the old homestead's barn. Little do the sisters suspect as they stock their shelves with Amish handcrafted gift items, antiques, and yummy baked goods that they're also filling the rustic store with a host of mysteries and surprises. Learn More

A perfect blend of faith, family and fun!

You'll get sneak peeks of new releases, recommendations from other Guideposts readers, and special offers just for you . . .

and it's FREE!

Just go to Guideposts.org/Newsletters today to sign up.

Guideposts.

Visit Guideposts.org/Shop or call (800) 932-2145

Find more inspiring stories in these best-loved Guideposts fiction series!

Mysteries of Lancaster County

Follow the Classen sisters as they unravel clues and uncover hidden secrets in Mysteries of Lancaster County. As you get to know these women and their friends, you'll see how God brings each of them together for a fresh start in life.

Secrets of Wayfarers Inn

Retired schoolteachers find themselves owners of an old warehouse-turned-inn that is filled with hidden passages, buried secrets, and stunning surprises that will set them on a course to puzzling mysteries from the Underground Railroad.

Tearoom Mysteries Series

Mix one stately Victorian home, a charming lakeside town in Maine, and two adventurous cousins with a passion for tea and hospitality. Add a large scoop of intriguing mystery, and sprinkle generously with faith, family, and friends, and you have the recipe for Tearoom Mysteries.

Ordinary Women of the Bible

Richly imagined stories—based on facts from the Bible—have all the plot twists and suspense of a great mystery, while bringing you fascinating insights on what it was like to be a woman living in the ancient world.

To learn more about these books, visit Guideposts.org/Shop